Tiny

Two best friends find love, happiness—and little bundles of joy!

Friends Fran and Kellie have been through thick and thin together since childhood, and now both are facing the fact that their dreams of motherhood might never happen.

Follow the two women's stories as they fall in love with two gorgeous Greeks and find happiness beyond their wildest dreams—as well as the little longed-for miracles they never thought possible....

Available in February, read Fran's story:
BABY OUT OF THE BLUE

Available in April, read Kellie's story:
ALONG CAME TWINS...

Dear Reader,

Along Came Twins... is the second book in my series Tiny Miracles. In my first book, *Baby out of the Blue,* the heroine had to deal with the problem of never being able to give birth to a baby. In this second book, the heroine must go through artificial insemination in order to try and get pregnant—but all seems hopeless.

In real life, one of my dear sisters and her husband adopted two precious babies. Then lo and behold, maybe ten years later, she found herself pregnant—and a year later was pregnant again. They now have four precious children. Our family considers *those* babies miracles!

I'd like to dedicate this book to my sister Heather and all those would-be mothers waiting for their own miracles to happen.

Enjoy!

Rebecca Winters

REBECCA WINTERS

Along Came Twins...

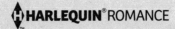

HARLEQUIN® ROMANCE

ISBN-13: 978-0-373-74238-7

ALONG CAME TWINS...

First North American Publication 2013

Printed in U.S.A.

Rebecca Winters, whose family of four children has now swelled to include five beautiful grandchildren, lives in Salt Lake City, Utah, in the land of the Rocky Mountains. With canyons and high alpine meadows full of wildflowers, she never runs out of places to explore. They, plus her favorite vacation spots in Europe, often end up as backgrounds for her romance novels, because writing is her passion, along with her family and church.

Rebecca loves to hear from readers. If you wish to email her, please visit her website, www.cleanromances.com.

Books by Rebecca Winters

BABY OUT OF THE BLUE
THE COUNT'S CHRISTMAS BABY
ACCIDENTALLY PREGNANT!
THE NANNY AND THE CEO
HER DESERT PRINCE
AND BABY MAKES THREE
HER ITALIAN SOLDIER
A BRIDE FOR THE ISLAND PRINCE
THE RANCHER'S HOUSEKEEPER

Other titles by this author available in ebook format.

CHAPTER ONE

"DR. SAVAKIS? THANK YOU for seeing me at the end of your busy day. When Dr. Creer, my doctor in Philadelphia, told me I was pregnant with twins, no one could have been more surprised than I was. You wouldn't know that since my last visit to you before I left Athens, I filed for divorce. It will be final in a few days."

Her fertility doctor shook his balding head. "After such a joyous outcome, what a pity, Mrs. Petralia. I remember how excited you both were to know your allergy problem didn't have to interfere with your ability to conceive. Now that you're pregnant, I'm extremely sorry to hear this news."

No one could be sorrier than she was, but she didn't want to discuss it. "I still need to tell my husband, but it isn't the kind of thing he should hear over the phone. That's why I'm here in Greece for a few days."

"I see."

"I wanted to pay you a visit to let you know the procedure worked. After all we went through together, naturally I wanted to give you my personal thanks." Her voice caught. "It's been a dream of mine to have a baby. Despite my failed marriage, I'm ecstatic over this pregnancy. Leandros will be thrilled, too. As you know, his first wife died carrying their unborn child, and he lost them both. Without your help, this miracle would never have happened."

She should have gone to Leandros first with the news, but decided that by coming to their doctor to tell him her marriage was over, it would make the divorce more real somehow and help her to face Leandros.

Dr. Savakis eyed her soberly through his bifocals. "I'm glad for you and pleased you phoned to see me. How are you feeling?"

"Since the doctor prescribed pills that help my nausea, I'm much better."

He smiled. "Good. You'll need to take extra care of yourself now."

"I know. I plan to, believe me."

"As long as you're here, I have information that might interest you at some later date."

"What is it?"

"More medical research has been done on your condition. Did your doctor tell you?"

"No. I've only seen him once."

"He'll no doubt discuss this with you during one of your appointments with him."

Kellie thought about all the anguish she'd been through hoping to get pregnant. "It doesn't matter now. I'm going to have my hands full raising my twins."

"Nothing could make me happier in that regard. But you need to keep in mind what I'm telling you for the future. You're only twenty-eight. In time you could find yourself remarried and wanting another child."

She shook her head. "No, Dr. Savakis. That part of my life is over." Though they hadn't been able to make their marriage work, Leandros had spoiled her for other men. He'd been the great love of her life. There would never be another.

"You say that now, but one never knows what the future will bring."

"I—I appreciate that," she stammered, "but I can't think about anything else except raising my children."

"I understand," he said kindly. "If you have any problems while you're here in Athens, call me. There's a Dr. Hanno on staff here who's an OB and works with high-risk patients. If you're going to be in Greece for any length of time, I'd advise you to call him and make an appointment for a checkup. Tell him I referred you. And don't forget. I'm always at your disposal."

"Thank you, Dr. Savakis. You've been wonderful. I want you to know I'll always be grateful."

Kellie left his office in the medical building attached to the hospital and took a taxi back to the Civitel Olympic Hotel in central Athens. She was exhausted and hungry. Tomorrow morning she'd approach her soon-to-be ex-husband, wherever he happened to be. Her breath caught just thinking about seeing him again. It was better for her mind not to go there.

Once she had dinner in her room, she'd phone her aunt and uncle to let them know she'd arrived safely.

It was after eleven at night when the door connecting Leandros's office with his private secretary's opened. Everyone had gone home six hours go. It was probably one of the security guards, but he still resented the interruption.

He looked up to discover his sister-in-law on her way in with a tray of food in hand.

A scowl broke out on his face. "What are you doing here, Karmela?"

"Mrs. Kostas told me you'd be working through the night to get ready for your mysterious trip. Is it true you're leaving in the morning?"

"That's not your concern."

"I thought you'd like a cup of coffee and some sandwiches to help you stay awake." She put it on his desk.

"You should have gone home with everyone else. I'm not hungry and need total quiet to work through these specs."

"Well, I'm here now." She grabbed a sandwich and sank into one of the chairs near his desk to eat. "Don't be grumpy. I worry about you. So do Mom and Dad. They've tried to get you to come to dinner, but you keep turning them down."

"I've been busy."

"Where are you going on your vacation?"

"That's confidential."

"I'm family, remember? I like to do things for you."

"You need to lead your own life. I appreciate the coffee, but now you have to go."

She didn't budge. "You shouldn't have married Kellie. She wasn't good enough for you, you know."

His hands curled into fists. Before Kellie had shut the door on him in Philadelphia, she'd expressed the same sentiment to him. He'd been crushed that she would even think such a thing, let alone say it to his face.

But for Karmela to dare speak her mind like this made him furious. She was never one to worry about boundaries. His first wife, Petra, had warned him about it and had asked him to overlook that flaw in her sister.

Unfortunately, tonight Karmela had stepped over a line he couldn't forgive. Something wasn't right with his sister-in-law. He recalled the times Kellie had made a quiet comment about Karmela's familiarity with him. *And how many times did you brush it off as unimportant, Petralia?*

He fought to control his temper, but it was wearing thin. "You've said enough."

"Ooh. You really are upset." She got up from the chair. "The only reason I came in here was to help you." Tears filled her eyes. "You used to let me when Petra was alive." *Only because Petra asked me to be kind to you.* "I miss her and know you do, too."

He'd had all he could tolerate. "Leave *now*!"

"Okay. I'm going."

"Take the tray with you." He kept the coffee.

At the door she turned to him. "How long will you be gone?"

"I have no idea. In any event, it's no one's business but mine."

"Why are you being so hurtful?"

"Why do you continually go where angels fear to tread?" he retorted without looking at her. "Good night. Lock the door on your way out."

Relieved when the sound of her footsteps faded, he got back to work. In the morning he'd call Frato and go over the most important items before he took off. His eyes fastened on the picture of Kellie that sat on his desk. He was living to see his golden-blond wife again. Though they'd both hurt each other, he'd do whatever it took to get her back.

When Kellie awakened the next morning, she was so nervous to see Leandros again, she decided it was a mistake to have come to Athens. The talk with Dr. Savakis had opened up thoughts and feelings she'd been trying to suppress.

Soon after their wedding she'd been diagnosed with a semen allergy, but the doctor had said he saw no reason why they couldn't get pregnant. She and Leandros went to their first artificial insemination appointment with such high hopes. Kellie wanted a baby with him desperately. He was eager for it, too, and had made certain his business matters didn't interfere while they went through the steps necessary for conception to work.

Leandros had been so sweet and tender with her about their situation. Like any happily married couple wanting to start a family, they'd waited for the signs that meant she had conceived. Two months into their marriage, her period came. Leandros had kissed her and loved her out of her disappointment.

"Next month," he'd whispered.

Knowing he was disappointed, too, she'd loved him back with all the energy in her, wanting to show him she wouldn't allow this to dampen her spirits. Once again they went back to the hospital, for another try, only to be disappointed the following month.

So many tries full of expectations, but each waiting period had seemed harder than the last, contributing to the problems that had slowly crept into their marriage. What bit-

tersweet irony that now they were divorcing,
she was pregnant.

After she showered and got dressed, she
phoned for a breakfast tray. Halfway through
her meal she panicked. What she ought to do
was go right back to Pennsylvania and phone
him when there were thousands of miles between them. But it would be the cowardly
thing to do. Her aunt and uncle never said as
much, but she knew they'd be disappointed in
her if she left it to a phone call.

You have to tell him.

You can't leave it up to anyone else.

Whatever is ultimately decided about the
children, he has the right to hear it from you
in person.

All the voices speaking in Kellie's head finally drove her to follow through with her
agenda.

She asked the front desk to phone for a
taxi. In a few minutes she found herself being
driven along Kifissias Avenue toward the Petralia Corporation office building in down-
town Athens. When it pulled up in front, she
paid the driver and got out.

After taking a deep breath, she squared her
shoulders and opened the doors, where Giorgios, looking like a well-dressed prizefighter,

sat at the security desk near the entry. When he saw her, he shot to his feet in surprise.

"*Kyria Petralia*—"

Her chocolate-brown eyes fastened on him. He was one of Leandros's bodyguards and fiercely loyal to him. "Good morning, Giorgios. It's nice to see you. Is my husband on the premises?"

"He arrived an hour ago."

The news relieved her, since she hadn't relished the thought of trying to hunt Leandros down. He could have been out of the city doing business right now. Then again, he could have been at his apartment here in Athens, or at his villa on the family estate on Andros.

"If you still want a job with him, you won't let him or Christos know I'm here," she said in fluent Greek.

His expression turned to shock before Kellie walked around his desk to the elevator located behind him. Unless Leandros made a helicopter landing on the roof after his flight from Andros Island, the elevator existed for his exclusive use when he entered or left the building from the street. For convenience sake it opened to the foyer of his private inner sanctum on the top floor. Giorgios had orders to guard it with his life.

She pressed her hand to the glass by the door, wondering if it would still recognize her code. For all she knew, Leandros had deleted it. But no, the door opened. She entered, still feeling Giorgios's stunned gaze on her before it closed.

A little over a month ago she'd left Greece, vowing never to return. But a week ago nausea had driven her to make an appointment with her doctor in Philadelphia. When he told her what was wrong with her, a transformation had taken place inside Kellie. It transcended the anguish and pain of the past year and gave her the spine she needed to face Leandros one more time.

Their divorce would soon be final. She intended for nothing to change in that regard, but since this totally unexpected contingency had arisen, it required an alteration in the documents their two lawyers had drawn up. Twenty-four hours should give Leandros's attorney enough time to take care of the necessary changes.

Kellie was desperate to catch her husband off guard; it was the only way to get through this final ordeal with him. She dreaded it, knew it would hurt, but had no other choice. For that reason she hadn't even told her best friend, Fran Meyers, she was coming.

Fran was now married to Nikolos Angelis, a good friend of Leandros's. They lived here in Athens with Nik's baby niece, Demi, soon-to-be their adopted daughter. If Nik knew of her arrival, he'd have phoned Leandros. Among the legal papers in her purse was evidence of the restraining order she'd placed on Leandros to call off her bodyguard. Yannis had been her shadow for the two years she'd been married to Leandros. But when she'd demanded a divorce, she'd drawn the line at the retired secret service agent following her to the States. Leandros had been forced to comply, with the result that he had no prior knowledge she'd flown to Athens yesterday.

As the elevator carried her skyward, Kellie planned to take care of business as quickly as possible. She knew she'd soon be on her way back home to Philadelphia, where she'd been living with her aunt and uncle for the last month. But that was about to change.

By next week she'd move her aunt and uncle from their small apartment into a lovely four-bedroom brick row home in Parkwood with her. It was a charming residential neighborhood in the far northeast corner of Philadelphia, perfect for children. She'd already put down a deposit. A new life awaited her, but first things first.

When the elevator stopped and the door opened, Kellie took a deep breath and headed through the foyer. She walked past Christos, her husband's chief bodyguard. He started to reach for his phone to warn Leandros, but she put a finger to her lips and smiled. He nodded and sat down again.

A few more steps and she reached the entrance to her husband's private suite, which was also protected by a security code. As CEO of the Petralia Corporation, which built resorts all over Greece, he was one of the most successful businessmen in the country and had been a target for crazies long before Kellie had met him.

She had no idea what she might be interrupting, but that wasn't her concern anymore. It had been on her wedding day, two years ago, when Kellie realized she had an enemy in Karmela Paulos. Karmela was the sister of Petra, Leandros's first wife, who'd been pregnant when she'd died in a plane crash. At Kellie's wedding to Leandros, the beautiful, fashionable Karmela would willingly have scratched Kellie's eyes out if she could have gotten away with it.

Fran had been Kellie's matron of honor and had witnessed the obvious fact that Karmela had hoped to become the next Mrs. Leandros Petralia. But it didn't happen, so his sister-in-law had done the next best thing by becoming indispensable to Leandros, first as a confidante to the grieving widower, who was family, and later as a secretary in his inner office, under Mrs. Kostas. With cunning, Karmela had worked her way to the top floor, where she had daily contact with him.

Combined with the stress Kellie had been under because she couldn't conceive, plus her struggle with feelings of inadequacy, the situation had grown intolerable for her. After much thought and soul-searching, she'd told Leandros she wanted a separation, and had left on a trip with Fran. But because of disastrous circumstances, it came to an abrupt end, with her friend staying in Athens to be with Nik. At that point Kellie had left for Philadelphia.

On the night before she was due to fly back, she'd had a fainting spell and Leandros had taken her to the ER. When the doctor could find nothing wrong, she was sent home with the warning to eat, so it wouldn't happen again. They'd just returned when Karmela, whose hand was obviously recognized by the security entry, slipped into their apartment, as she'd done when Petra still lived there.

The fact that Leandros said nothing about his sister-in-law letting herself in unannounced had led Kellie to worry that he had more than brotherly feelings for Karmela. After all, she did resemble Petra. Perhaps, as Kellie had confided to Fran earlier, Karmela had become his pillow friend?

Evidently his brazen sister-in-law figured she had free reign with Leandros now that Kellie was leaving him. Her smiling, catlike eyes stared boldly at Kellie as she explained she'd brought some work for Leandros that needed his attention. Before she slipped out the door again, she'd wished Kellie a safe flight back to the States. No doubt she thought she'd seen the last of her. Kellie knew that her presence would knock the daylights out of Karmela, but this wasn't about her. It was about them—Leandros and Kellie—and their babies.

She put her palm against the glass next to the door. She suspected Karmela's manipulative smile would falter when Kellie walked into the office and word eventually circulated about the miraculous news. Everyone close to Leandros knew he'd mourned the loss of his first wife and unborn child, who would have been a girl.

Despite Kellie's impending divorce from Leandros, for him to learn he was going to be a father again would come as a tremendous thrill. But it would deal a near fatal blow to his sister-in-law's plans to have him for her own.

Kellie knew in her heart that Karmela was waiting for her chance to provide him with a living heir. At least that's what Frato Petralia had confided to Kellie at the wedding, after having too much to drink.

Frato was Leandros's good-looking first cousin and closest friend in the family. Still single, he was one of the vice presidents of the corporation, and enjoyed the company of several beautiful women, which didn't surprise Kellie at all. That evening he'd said quite a few things she didn't take seriously in the beginning, but over time she realized he'd spoken the truth.

On the day Leandros mentioned in passing about hiring Karmela to work under Mrs. Kostas, she'd tried not to let it affect her. But her first impression of Petra's sister at the wedding wouldn't leave her alone. She'd seen the way Karmela had behaved and talked to him. Karmela was no impartial bystander. Two years later the younger woman had insinuated herself into Leandros's office life, and who knew how much more. But it was all history now.

The elevator door opened silently along the wall away from his desk. Leandros sat in his swivel chair, half turned from her while engaged in an intense business discussion with Frato on the speakerphone. She recognized his voice.

At first glance she realized Leandros needed a haircut and a shave. There were wavy tendrils of dark hair, a shade away from being true black, clinging to his bronzed nape. It looked as if he'd been running his hands through it. The sleeves of the white shirt he wore had been pushed up to the elbows. Given his condition, and the accumulation of coffee cups on the desk, she could imagine he might have spent the night here.

She'd never seen him like this before. He was thirty-four, yet he looked five years older right now. Her normally fastidious, temperate husband was nowhere to be found. Kellie had seen him truly out of control only once before. It was the night she'd told him she wanted a divorce. In a way, this was worse— different, even—because there was a savage air about him. For a second she feared she'd done the wrong thing by coming here without his knowledge. But with so much riding on this, she couldn't run from him now. Too much was at stake.

Finding her courage, she called out softly to him. "Leandros?"

She knew he'd heard her voice, because his hard, lean body seemed to freeze in place before he slowly swung around to face her.

He'd lost weight. A pronounced white ring encircled his taut mouth, testifying to his incredulity at seeing her here. It stood out almost as much as his gray eyes, which had gone black as pitch at the moment. Their color reminded her of the dark sky before the tornado had struck the Petralia resort near Thessalonika five weeks ago, killing little Demi's parents.

Frato was on the other end of the phone line, still talking. Leandros muttered something she couldn't understand, before he hung up. His haunted look sent a shiver of alarm through her body. She sensed he was ready to spring from his chair.

"Don't get up," she urged, and walked over to one of the chairs in front of his desk to sit down. Not only had her legs turned to mush at the sight of him, she couldn't handle him touching her. He was still the most gorgeous man she'd ever known. In that regard, nothing had changed.

Kellie heard his sharp intake of breath. "What in the name of all that's holy brings you back to Greece?" His deep voice sounded so shaken, she hardly recognized it. His overarching look of disbelief sent a fresh shock wave of despair through her. The month apart had done the rest of the damage to their marriage, crushing the rubble to microscopic bits.

Suddenly there was a tap on the door and Karmela started to enter. "Not now!" Leandros snapped. Kellie had to admit she'd never seen Leandros this upset with an employee. Maybe he hadn't even realized it was Karmela.

Kellie was shocked by the other woman's sangfroid before she did Leandros's bidding. She was tall enough to wear the attractive black-and-white dress skimming her figure. With her hair falling like a silky black curtain, she was extraordinarily beautiful and would cause a traffic jam when she walked down the street.

Since she and Petra shared such a strong resemblance, Kellie could well imagine how his former wife had turned the sought-after bachelor into a married man. Karmela's hourglass figure was so different from Kellie's rounded curves.

The younger woman closed the door, but not before she shot Kellie a venomous glance. That reaction alone vindicated Kellie's belief that Karmela planned to win Leandros one way or another, if she hadn't already.

"Karmela still works for you, I see. And is still dropping in unannounced. As I recall, the last time we thought we were alone, Karmela dropped by with some papers for you. Though she didn't find us making love, she certainly *could* have if we hadn't been on the verge of divorce."

That was the first time Kellie had truly feared Leandros had been unfaithful to her with Karmela. Before that time, she'd only worried about the other woman's behavior.

"She was wrong to have done that, Kellie."

"It certainly was wrong, but you didn't say so at the time. I was so hurt when you let her come to work for you, and I told you as much, but you kept her on. We're almost divorced, yet she *still* works for you. As I've told you many times, your sister-in-law always had a habit of insinuating herself around you.

"Even a little while ago she walked in without as much as a tap on the door, but it's all right with you because *she's family.*"

Why did she sound so bitter? Kellie wondered. It was no longer her concern what Karmela did with Leandros. They were getting divorced. But the thought that he'd replaced her so soon hurt more than she could ever admit.

His beautiful olive complexion darkened with lines. "It's never been all right with me and I *am* going to do something about it. I'll ask you again. Why are you here?" He seemed to have lost some color.

Clearing her throat, she said, "I have news that demanded I come here in person." She was in possession of certain facts that would alter his world forever.

His hooded gaze pierced hers. "Has something happened to your aunt or uncle?"

Kellie could understand why he'd asked that question. He'd been wonderful to them from the moment he'd first met them. "This has nothing to do with them. They're fine."

She moistened her lips nervously. "A week ago I was so nauseated, I went to the doctor in Philadelphia to find out what was wrong. I learned that I'm...pregnant."

His dark head reared back in complete shock. "*What* did you say?" She heard excitement exploding inside him before he'd even had time to assimilate the news. Though he'd never given up hope they would get pregnant, Kellie had stopped believing such a miracle would happen to them.

She breathed in deeply. "I'm more amazed than you. It seems that the last artificial insemination procedure I underwent *worked*. Impossible as it sounds, Dr. Creer says I'm already seven weeks pregnant."

A triumphant cry escaped Leandros. He leaped out of his chair, charged with an energy that transformed him before her eyes. Her pulse raced, because she'd known this would be his reaction. "The doctor said it's the reason I fainted the night before I left Athens. My periods have never been normal, so I never suspected anything."

Leandros came around and hunkered down in front of her, like a knight kneeling before his lady. When he grasped her hands, she could feel him trembling. Emotion had taken the blackness from his eyes, filling the gray irises with pinpoints of light. "We're going to have a baby?" There was awe in his voice as he kissed her fingertips. The news had started to sink in, but he didn't know all of it yet.

"There's more, Leandros."

Fear immediately marred his striking features and his hands gripped hers tighter. "Did the doctor tell you you're a high-risk pregnancy? Is something wrong?"

"No," she rushed to assure him. After he'd lost his first wife and unborn child, she didn't want to put him through such anxiety again. He didn't deserve any more trauma in that regard.

His expressive black brows furrowed. "Then what *do* you mean?"

Averting her eyes, she said, "The doctor ordered an ultrasound."

"And?" His voice shook.

"The technician detected two heartbeats."

"Two?" His explosion of joy reverberated off the walls of his office. "We're going to have twins?"

She nodded. "They're due March 12."

"Kellie—"

The next thing she knew he'd picked her up and wrapped her in his strong arms, burying his face in her neck. She felt moisture against her skin as he crushed her against him. He'd been at the hospital with her to do his part while they'd gone through procedure after procedure. Every time it turned out she hadn't gotten pregnant, he'd been there to comfort her and promise her it would happen next time. He never gave up, and now they were going to be parents. But it was too late for them. The situation had put too much strain on both of them.

His reaction to the news was all she could have wanted if they'd been happily married, but that was the excruciating point. Their marriage was over and had been for months.

Soon they'd be divorced. Having his babies wouldn't solve what was wrong between them. When he lifted his head to kiss her, she put her hands against his chest to separate them, but he wasn't having any of it.

"Don't push me away, *agapi mou*. Not now," he cried. Before she could move, he drew her back into his arms and lowered his mouth to hers, kissing her with startling hunger. She could taste the salt from his tears. Her mind and body reeled from the passion only he could arouse.

For a moment she responded, because it had

been so long since she'd known his touch, and because she simply couldn't help herself. But when he moaned and deepened their kiss, she remembered why she was here.

Since he was physically powerful, her only weapon was to refrain from kissing him back until he got the message. He went on kissing every inch of her face and hair till it slowly dawned on him she was no longer participating.

A tremor shook his tall, hard-muscled body before he released her with reluctance. Dazed by his passion, she sank down in the chair behind her. His eyes searched her features, trying to read her. "Are you still suffering from morning sickness?"

"No," she answered honestly. Though she'd love to use it as an excuse, she couldn't. From here on out, everything she told him would be the whole truth and out in the open.

Dr. Creer was very worried about her going through a divorce right now. He'd warned her that since she didn't want to burden her aunt and uncle with her problems, then she needed to find an outlet to deal with all her emotions. Keeping them bottled up inside was the worst thing for her at a time like this. She could tell Dr. Savakis had been worried about her, too.

After being alone with her thoughts for the last month, she realized the doctor was right. She'd gone about things wrong in her marriage. She was sick of trying to protect herself, Leandros and everyone else. But no longer. No more mistakes if she could help it. That's why she'd come all this way. "The doctor has given me medication for it."

His hands went to his hips, as if he needed to do something with them. Unfortunately, he stood too close to her, affecting her breathing. "This pregnancy puts a different slant on our impending divorce."

"I know. That's one of the reasons I'm here."

"You do realize that a great deal of our pain came from trying to get pregnant without results," he reminded her grimly.

"So now that I'm carrying your child, you think that erases everything?"

"No," he murmured, "but you've just brought me news I'm still trying to assimilate. One moonlit night on the sailboat, after we'd been disappointed a second time, you lifted tear-filled eyes to me and asked me if it was asking too much to reach for the stars. I told you we'd keep reaching for the stars and the moon. Now you've just told me we've been given *both*!"

"I remember." She averted her eyes. "Please sit down so we can talk."

Studying her through veiled eyes, he hitched himself on a corner of his desk. It still wasn't far enough away from her, but that was as much room as he was willing to give her. "I have a better idea. We'll go to our suite at the hotel, where we won't be disturbed."

He was referring to the Cassandra, the main Petralia five-star hotel in Athens, where he kept an elegant, permanent suite. It was like a small house, really, with three bedrooms, a dining and living room and kitchen facilities.

When she'd stayed at the hotel with her aunt and uncle on their first trip to Greece, that's where she'd met him. Some of her happiest memories of their life together were associated with the Cassandra before they were married. It would be painful to go there.

"Why do we have to go to the hotel? Why not the apartment?"

He moved off the corner of the desk. "We can't go to the apartment because I sold it to Frato three weeks ago. I'm living at the hotel."

CHAPTER TWO

LEANDROS HAD SOLD his fabulous penthouse to his cousin? Kellie couldn't believe it. Stunned by the news, she said, "What's to stop Karmela from hurrying over to the hotel with something important for you before the day is out?"

He breathed in sharply. "It'll never happen again."

Kellie blinked. "That sounded final. She must have received quite a shock to see me in here with you a few minutes ago, but no worries. I won't be in Athens much longer."

In the tangible silence that followed, Kellie lowered her eyes and opened her purse. Inside was the paper her attorney had drawn up. "If you'll please read through this and consult with your attorney, then we'll sign it and our divorce can go through as scheduled."

Leandros made no move to take it. She should have known this was going to be a battle to the end. "That's all right. I'll read it to you.

"Point One. If and when one or both children are born, the mother will retain custody at her address in Parkwood, Pennsylvania."

"Why *if*?" he demanded in an anxious voice. "Is there something you haven't told me?"

"No. My attorney simply wanted to cover every contingency."

Shadows darkened his features.

"Point Two. Liberal visitation rights will be offered to the father.

"Point Three. Both mother and father will discuss times when the mother will bring said child or children to Athens for visitation, and when the father will travel to Parkwood for visitation.

"Point Four. The mother asks for no additional money. The father can decide what monies he will afford for the child or children's upbringing."

She looked up at him. "It's all very simple and straightforward."

His eyes glittered a frostbite gray. "If you think I'm going to agree to that, then you never knew me." The words seemed to come from a cavern miles underground.

"You're wrong, Leandros. After being married for a while, I discovered the *real* you. That's why we've reached this impasse." Heartbroken, she stood up and left the paper on his desk.

With a grimace, he immediately wadded it in his fist before pocketing it. "When did you fly in?"

"Yesterday morning. I'm staying at the Civitel Olympic near the north park. You can reach me there after you've talked with your attorney."

Leandros moved like lightning, preventing her from leaving the room. Standing in front of the door, he talked into his cell phone and rapped out instructions. When he clicked off, he said, "You won't be going back to the Civitel. I'll send Yannis for your personal belongings and have him bring them to you. We're flying to Andros right now."

Where else would he take her? It was his favorite place on earth. *Hers, too, except...* "You mean where Karmela and her family drop in on a regular basis to visit your family whenever you're in residence there?"

His eyes narrowed to slits. "They come to visit my parents in their villa. As for my family, they've already left for the yearly reunion in Stenies village and will be gone overnight, so no one will be around. In any case, we'll be staying in my villa. Shall we go?"

So much had happened in the last month, Kellie's mind was spinning. Since he'd dictated the location for the conversation they needed to have, she was left with no choice but to go along with him.

After grabbing his briefcase, he opened the door that led to the elevator, and stepped in behind her. Their bodies brushed, sending darts of awareness through her as they rode to the roof, where the helicopter blades were already rotating.

She smiled at his pilot, Stefon, before climbing in the back to join Christos. Kellie had done this so often in the past, she strapped herself in before Leandros could do it. She watched him take the copilot's seat and put on the earphones. Soon they were airborne for the short flight to Andros, an hour and a half from Athens by car and ferry. There was no airport, but with a helicopter, Leandros could be where he wanted in no time at all.

That pang of familiarity attacked her in waves as they left Athens and headed for the fertile green island in the Cyclades that Leandros called home. It was a contrast of craggy mountains, woods, valleys and streams rising out of the blue Aegean.

The Petralia estate was located on the eastern slope of a hillside with its share of vineyards, lemon and walnut groves near Gialia beach. To Kellie, the island was glorious beyond description.

Close by was the picturesque stone village of Stenies, with its paved streets. The cluster of villas on the estate had been built in the same traditional stone architecture of the region. Parents, grandparents, uncles and aunts, cousins...all lived in the vicinity.

Leandros loved it because tourism hadn't been developed in this quieter area, thus preserving the whole place's authentic character. After their wedding, at the church in Chora, Kellie had thought she'd found paradise on her honeymoon here, until she learned the Paulos family, among other wealthy families, lived on the same part of the island. The two families had enjoyed a warm relationship over the last fifty years.

Once she'd realized this was where Leandros had fallen in love with Petra, Kellie never felt as excited when they flew over on the weekends he didn't have a business commitment elsewhere. To her growing discomfort, she'd often discovered Karmela and her parents were there visiting Leandros's family at his parents' villa. They would always call Leandros and ask him to join them. Their presence had to be a reminder of what he'd lost.

Since his feelings for home were intertwined with his memories of Petra, Kellie imagined he was a prisoner of both. To fight her pain, she'd preferred they stay at the apartment in Athens when she wasn't traveling with him on business.

Now there was no apartment, but none of that mattered at this point. Wherever Leandros took her so they could talk, nothing would change the fact that they were getting a divorce, children or no children. There were some things they just couldn't overcome, no matter how much her heart broke at the thought.

She'd done the right thing by coming to him with the news of his impending fatherhood. It was his God-given right. If he found a way to prevent the divorce from happening as soon as she'd anticipated, she would still go back to Pennsylvania day after tomorrow, and let her attorney deal with it.

While she was deep in thought, Stefon flew them over the capital town of Chora, where the tourists came in throngs to see its charming Venetian architecture. Farther on she spotted the seventeenth century tower of Bisti-Mouvela and the nearby church of Agios Georgios. Soon they were passing over the Petralia estate. It was a wonderful place with an old olive press building, all part of Leandros's idyllic childhood and an intrinsic part of who he was.

The first time Kellie ever saw his romantic stone farmhouse with its flat roof, she'd fallen instantly in love with it. When she stayed there with him, she enjoyed the many terraces planted with fruit and nut trees that flourished in the climate, as well as shrubs, flowers and kitchen gardens. Hidden in the foliage was a small swimming pool.

One of her favorite features was the kitchen with its open fireplace. They could eat on two of the terraces, one alcoved between the kitchen and living room, the other above the master bedroom with its own garden and a view of the beach just steps away. Farther along the beach was the private boat dock housing various watercraft, including the sailboat he'd given her. One thing she'd learned early: Leandros loved the water and swam like a fish.

She thought about the babies growing inside her. After they were born, they'd enjoy this legacy from their father. When they came on visitation, they'd become water babies, too. But their roots would be firmly planted in Philadelphia.

There couldn't be two places on earth more unalike. Almost as unalike as the way she and Leandros viewed their marriage and what was wrong with it. Kellie couldn't bear to look back at what had happened to destroy their happiness, and fought tears as Stefon set them down on the east side of his parents' villa.

Leandros was already removing his headset. Now that she was pregnant, she had to expect that he would watch over her with meticulous care for the short time she was back in Greece. He didn't know any other way. That was one of the reasons she loved him so much.

Too much.

As he helped her down from the helicopter, his pulse raced to see moisture glazing those velvety brown eyes that used to beg him to make love to her. Until this minute, Leandros hadn't seen a sign of emotion from his normally loving, vivacious wife.

Since Kellie had first told him she wanted a separation, she'd turned into an ice princess, erecting walls he couldn't penetrate. For the last month they were together, he hadn't been able to get through to her on any level. The hurt he'd felt had turned to anger.

During the months when she'd gone through one procedure after another to get pregnant, and been so brave about it, they'd both felt the strain. Every time her period came, they both suffered depression and had to fight their way out of it.

Sometimes the strain made them short with each other. Other times there were periods of silence over several days. The emotional turmoil took its toll. By the last month, he didn't feel he knew his wife anymore. His disillusionment was so total, he'd been devastated.

Only the pregnancy could have caused her to venture back here. Though he was euphoric to learn he was going to be a father, his world would never be right again if the divorce went through without one more attempt to try and heal their wounds.

That's why he'd planned to leave today, with a proposition to save their marriage before it became final. For her to have flown here with news of their babies had saved him from flying to Philadelphia. Leandros couldn't have asked for a greater gift than her presence right now.

While the men disappeared to the guest cottage, she walked ahead of him, strolling down the flower-lined path to his villa in her pale orange sundress and jacket. His eyes followed the feminine lines of her hips and legs as she moved. In the summery outfit, his wife took his breath away.

Once upon a time they'd paused and kissed as they made their way along the ancient paths. But he had to push those rapturous memories to the background of his mind and start over with her again in a brand-new way.

Kellie waited for him to unlock the door, then stepped past him into the beamed living room with its simple white walls and hand-carved furniture. Her arm brushed against his, triggering a surge of desire for her with an intensity that caught him off guard. They'd been apart too long.

He set down his briefcase. "Why don't you rest on the couch by the window and I'll get us something cold to drink."

"Thank you."

When he returned a minute later with an icy lemon fruit drink for her, he found her seated on one end of the sofa, staring out at the beach. He handed her the glass. "Wouldn't you like to put your legs up? Since we're having twins, I'm sure the doctor told you to stay off your feet after your long flight from Philadelphia."

"You're right, but I had a good night's sleep at the hotel and ate breakfast in bed before I took a taxi to your office." She sipped her drink. "It's a hot day and this tastes wonderful. Thank you." Her controlled civility was anathema to him.

"You're welcome. When you're hungry, I'll fix us some sandwiches."

"I'm fine for now, but you go ahead."

He frowned. "I haven't had an appetite lately, but I can't claim the excuse of pregnancy." It wasn't meant to be a joke and she didn't take it that way. "How are you feeling physically?"

She avoided looking at him. "Dr. Creer says I'm in great shape. No problems in sight so far, but twins require special monitoring and I intend following his advice."

"That's good. Are you taking any other medicine besides your antinausea medication?"

"Just prenatal vitamins."

He drank part of his drink, then got to his feet, too restless to sit there. "When you walked in my office, I was on the phone with Frato."

"I know. I recognized his voice."

Leandros stared at her moodily. "He's taking over for me while I'm gone."

That statement caused her to lift startled eyes to him. "Where are you going?"

"I told him I needed a vacation, but no one knows my plans."

"You're taking another one?"

It didn't surprise him she'd ask that question. A month ago he'd taken time off to fly her back to Philadelphia. He was pleased to detect a note of concern in her voice before she smoothed her hands over her knees in what he recognized was a nervous gesture. "That's right."

"For how long this time?"

"For as long as it takes."

She stared at him. "I don't understand."

Leandros rubbed the back of his neck. "I was going to take my jet and fly to Philadelphia today to talk to you about giving us another chance. If you hadn't come to the office this morning, we would have missed each other."

Her eyes widened, then grew shuttered, and her lovely features hardened. "It's too late. Our divorce will be final soon. The fact that I'm pregnant changes nothing."

"I get that, Kellie, but I'd like you to hear me out first."

"What more is there to say?" The bleakness in her question crushed him. "I only came to discuss future visitation for our children and get it in writing."

He had to weigh his words carefully. "Our babies haven't arrived yet. Until they do, we have a lot to talk about that impacts our lives right this minute. What I need you to know is that I *did* listen to what you said to me before I flew home from Philadelphia a month ago. To my shame, it took me until last week to come to terms with it. I can't lose you, so I've made a decision that will affect both of us."

A troubled expression entered her eyes. "That sounds ominous."

He sucked in his breath. "I'm willing to do as you asked and go to marriage counseling with you."

Looking dumbstruck, she put her glass on the coffee table. "I thought you didn't believe in it. I brought up the subject a year ago, but you were adamantly against it."

He scowled in self-deprecation. "It's my nature to believe only in myself, but after being apart from you this last month, I recognize how arrogant that was of me. Since you suggested counseling as a last resort, I'm willing to try anything to save our marriage."

Besides her inability to get pregnant, which had tested them to the breaking point, there'd been other side issues throughout their marriage to exacerbate what was already wrong. One of them was Kellie's insistence that Karmela had a crush on him. Whenever she'd brought it up, he'd dismissed it, telling her Petra's sister was simply a clingy girl who needed lots of attention. Her behavior didn't mean anything. In fact, Petra had asked him to be extra kind to her.

But, he remembered, when Karmela had said last night that Kellie wasn't good enough for him, something in him had snapped. Mostly because in trying to do as Petra had asked, he hadn't taken Kellie's concerns seriously enough, he realized.

She got to her feet, as if on the verge of running away.

"I realize it will have to be someone you trust," he added, "so I want you to pick the therapist." Leandros knew this was a drastic departure from his former attitude, but he was desperate. Seeing her again proved to him he couldn't live without her. "We can do it here in Athens, or we can fly to Philadelphia and find someone there. It's your choice."

Without saying anything, she moved over to the French doors and opened them to walk out on the patio. He followed her, inhaling her flowery fragrance and the scent of the lemon trees close by. Incredible to think that inside her beautiful body, their babies were already seven weeks old and growing.

"Are you too embittered at this stage to even consider it, Kellie? I wouldn't blame you if you were...but I'm begging you."

She clung to the railing. Still no words came.

"I've spent the last week doing research on the best therapists in the city and came up with a list of six names recommended to me. Four men and two women. Let me show you."

He went back inside and reached for his briefcase. After pulling out his laptop, he set it up on the coffee table and turned it on. Kellie came back in and watched as he clicked to the file so she could see it.

"I was going to give you this list when I flew over to see you, but you can look at it now if you want. All the information I've gathered is here. But if this doesn't interest you, I'll fly you back to Philadelphia tomorrow and we'll search for a therapist there."

She shot him a startled glance. "You can't just go back and forth from Greece between sessions. Therapy takes time."

"I can do whatever I want. Frato will be running the company for as long as necessary. He knows the business the same as I do. With both our fathers still alive to advise him, along with other family members on the board, the company will function seamlessly. If you and I decide to do therapy in Philadelphia, then I'll live there and do business. With your help, of course."

"*My* help?"

"Yes. You once asked me if you could work for me. I told you I'd rather you didn't, but I was wrong about that and a host of other things. We can be a team and scout out a property for the first Petralia resort in Pennsylvania. But since you're pregnant, we'll have to proceed as your health dictates."

"You're not serious," she whispered.

"Try me and find out." He fired back the response. "We'll buy or build a house in Philadelphia near your aunt and uncle, if that's what you desire."

She shook her head. "And take you away from your family and responsibilities?"

"*You're* my family. No one else is more important. If we decide to live there, I'll step down as CEO."

"I wouldn't want or expect you to do that. Never!"

He stared into her eyes. "Why not? Don't you realize no place is home to me without you? I'll do anything, Kellie," he vowed. "I know we can make this work. It's not too late. For the sake of our unborn babies, I'm pleading with you to reconsider. If counseling will help us, then it will be worth it for all our sakes. We'll postpone our divorce while we're in therapy."

If Leandros had said these things to her a month ago...

But he's saying them to you now, Kellie.

For a proud man like her husband to be willing to undergo therapy told her how far he'd come. She moved closer to the coffee table, where she could see the list of names on his laptop. He'd done all this without prior knowledge that they were expecting twins? She couldn't believe it.

After supplying her this kind of proof that he was serious, she *had* to believe he'd planned to fly to Philadelphia today. But for Leandros to submit to marriage counseling... It just wasn't like him.

He was a dynamic wonder in the business world and a law unto himself. He'd probably last one session and that would be it. She couldn't imagine therapy working on him. But since she'd been the one to suggest it in the first place, how would it look if she told him no?

Kellie knew exactly what he'd think. During one of their arguments he'd told her she was inflexible, unreasonable and didn't really mean what she'd said. He would have every right to accuse her now of not putting their children first.

The more she thought about it, the more she realized the wisest thing to do would be to try out one of these therapists in Athens. When the counseling didn't work, then she'd fly back to Philadelphia and the divorce could go through. She'd have to let her aunt and uncle know. The news would be welcome to them, because they adored Leandros and were crushed by the news that he and Kellie were getting a divorce.

He watched as she sat down and scrolled through the list of names. All seemed to have impressive credentials. She was glad he'd included some women. She preferred their therapist to be a female, who would understand Kellie's point of view about things. Leandros probably wouldn't like it, but he'd said this was her choice.

She looked at their ages. The first woman was forty-eight, younger than Kellie's aunt. The other therapist was seventy-six. That sounded pretty old, but she did have a long record of running a practice. At that age she'd probably seen thousands of couples, with every type of problem, enter her office. To still be in business meant she'd enjoyed a certain amount of success.

"Today is a workday." Leandros's deep male voice permeated to Kellie's insides. "Is there a name on the list you'd like to call now?"

He stood behind the couch, more or less looking over her shoulder. Though he'd sounded in control just now, she sensed his impatience for their therapy to get started. Actually, she was anxious, too. The sooner they met with someone and discovered counseling wouldn't help, the sooner she could go home and start getting over Leandros once and for all.

"I'm rather impressed with this older woman, Olympia Lasko." She glanced back at him. "The notes say she's been in practice forty-five years. That's longer than any of the other therapists' histories. I think it speaks quite highly of her."

"I couldn't agree more. Go ahead and phone her."

Leandros didn't act the least upset with Kellie's choice. If he was, he'd learned how to hide his true feelings. That ability made him the shrewd genius who'd become one of the leading business figures in Greece.

She reached in her purse for her cell phone and made the call. It rang several times before a woman answered. "This is Olympia Lasko."

"Oh—" Kellie's voice caught. "I guess I expected a receptionist." She spoke in Greek.

"I've never used one. Your name, please."

"Kellie Petralia."

"What can I do for you?"

"M-my husband and I are on the verge of getting a divorce and need marriage counseling," she stammered. "Could I see you soon to discuss our situation, or are you too booked up?"

"Both of you come to my house tomorrow morning at ten o'clock."

"Both?" Kellie had planned to talk to her first and explain things.

"I never see you individually. It's together or nothing."

"I see." She bit her lip. "Then we'll both be there."

"What's your husband's name?"

"Leandros Petralia."

"Thank you. When you enter the driveway, keep going until you reach the side door. Just walk in."

The other woman rang off without making a remark about Kellie's husband. Ninety-nine percent of the time, people couldn't refrain from commenting on him and the famous Petralia name. Kellie sat there blinking in surprise.

Leandros walked around to look at her. "When can she see us?"

"Tomorrow at ten. We're to go to her house. She must work out of her home."

"Would that we all could do that," he murmured.

"I can't believe she had an opening this fast."

"My dentist always leaves the first hour

free for emergencies. It sounds like she operates the same way. I'm impressed already."

Kellie got up from the couch, unnerved by the prospect of talking to Mrs. Lasko in front of Leandros without any private time first. "She's very different than I'd supposed." No chitchat of any kind.

"Let's keep the appointment. If we decide she's not the one for us, then we'll try someone else."

Leandros was being so supportive, just as he'd always been during their visits to the hospital, that Kellie felt like screaming. But not at him. She was frightened, and nervous of being alone with him. "I think I'm hungry now."

"Why don't we drive to Chora and have an early dinner." He was reading her mind. She needed to be around other people and he knew it. "Do you have any particular cravings at this stage in your pregnancy?"

"Not yet."

"Let's try a restaurant you haven't been to. The Circe is on the far side of Chora. It's cozy and the cuisine is basically traditional Andriot." He'd probably been there with Petra. *Of course he had, you fool.* If the therapy didn't work out, Kellie would have to take part of the blame, because she couldn't rid herself of her demons. "You'll love their seafood mezes and froutalia."

"I've forgotten what froutalia is."

"A sensational omelet with sausage and other kinds of meat."

"Oh, yes. That sounds delicious."

"Good. Why don't you freshen up first. I'll meet you at the car parked around the side of the house."

"I'll hurry."

"There's no need. We have all the time in the world. By the time we get back, Yannis will have arrived with your luggage. You can have an early night in the guest bedroom."

Her heart ached as she realized how far apart they'd grown. No sleeping in the same bed for the past two months. Most likely never again...

When Kellie went outside a few minutes later, he was waiting for her, and helped her in the passenger side. She glanced at his striking profile as he started the engine. Whether immaculately groomed or disheveled with a five-o'clock shadow as he was now, Leandros's male beauty stood apart from other men's.

Her heart thudded ferociously. A month ago she'd never dreamed she'd be on the island with him again, going to a romantic spot for dinner.

During the six-mile drive to town, she stared out the window at the fruit trees dotting the ancient landscape. When she couldn't stand the silence any longer, she turned to him. "Have you seen Fran and Nik?"

He nodded. "They invited me to their apartment last week for dinner. Demi is thriving and has started to say words even I can understand." Kellie smiled. "I've never seen two people so happy."

Guilt washed over Kellie for the part she'd played in trying to influence Fran to stay away from the gorgeous Nik Angelis, Leandros's good friend. The press had labeled him Greece's number one playboy. Like Leandros, Nik was the head of his family's multimillion-dollar business and could have any woman he wanted.

In Kellie's zeal to protect her divorced friend's wounded heart, she'd done everything she could to get her away from Nik. She'd been convinced he would only use Fran. But it turned out Kellie was wrong. Ultimately, he'd proved to be the perfect man for her, and had married her on the spot. Since he couldn't give her children and she couldn't conceive, they were adopting Demi, who'd lost her parents in a tornado. In time they planned to adopt more.

"I'm so happy for them," Kellie said aloud.

"Me, too."

To Leandros's credit, he didn't rub it in about Kellie's behavior with her best friend before they'd flown to Philadelphia on his private jet. "I'll phone her while I'm here."

"She'll be delighted. Being a mother has turned a light on inside her."

You mean unlike me, who's pregnant but still wants the divorce?

Kellie wouldn't blame Leandros for thinking it, but again, he kept his thoughts to himself. That was the trouble between them. They were both festering in their own private way from behaviors that had driven them apart.

The therapist would have to perform a miracle for them to put their marriage back together. How ironic that Kellie had been the one who'd brought up the idea of counseling. Yet now that Leandros had finally agreed to it, she was only going through the motions. Deep inside she had no real hope of success.

There'd been too much damage done during those months of planning each hospital visit like clockwork. Everything had to be gauged down to the second—the temperature taking, the preparation, Leandros's time off from work…. All of it had affected the natural rhythm of married life.

If he suggested they skip a month of going to the hospital, and give things a rest, she was afraid he was losing interest in her. Maybe he didn't want a baby as badly as she did. When she asked him if he would still love her if she couldn't give him a child, he'd acted incensed, which in turn made her afraid to approach him again about it.

There were times when she'd feared he needed a break from her, and would tell him to enjoy a night out with friends or go visit his family. If he took her up on the suggestion, she cried herself to sleep. If he insisted on staying home with her, she feared it was out of a sense of duty. The spontaneity of their lives had vanished.

Aside from making sure she'd prepared a good meal for him at night, Kellie found herself spending more and more time playing tennis at Leandros's club with friends, or studying Greek with the tutor he'd hired for her at the university.

With the gulf so wide and deep between them because of what they'd gone through to have a baby, they were different people now.

Her heart ached, because she couldn't imagine how they could find their way back to the people they'd once been.

CHAPTER THREE

EARLY THE NEXT MORNING Stefon flew the two of them to the Cassandra in Athens. After eating breakfast in their room, Leandros called for his car and drove them to the Pangrati neighborhood, where Olympia Lasko saw her clients.

Silence filled the Mercedes, as it had last evening on their way home from dinner. Kellie had hardly talked to him and went straight to bed once they'd returned to the villa. If she'd gotten on the phone with Fran or her aunt and uncle, he knew nothing about it.

To his relief she'd eaten a healthy meal this morning and shown more appetite than he had. Leandros didn't know about Kellie, but he'd slept poorly. Not only was he concerned over the process they were about to undergo, he feared Kellie's reaction. Though it had been her idea, this was new territory for both of them.

After he'd dismissed the idea of counseling in the beginning, he was thankful that she was still willing to try it. When they'd reached Andros yesterday, he'd been terrified out of his mind she would tell him it was too late, and fly right back to Pennsylvania.

Before long, he turned the corner and spotted the Lasko home. It was a moderate-size, gray-and-white two-story house, typical of the settled, comfortable looking residences along the street in the quiet neighborhood. Leandros pulled in the driveway and stopped at the side entrance.

He eyed his wife, who, thankfully, was still his wife. He'd already contacted his attorney to get in touch with her attorney and put off the divorce. The only thing left was to follow through with counseling and pray for a breakthrough. "Shall we go in?"

She nodded and started to get out of the car. He hurried around to help her. Together they walked beneath the portico to the porch. "Mrs. Lasko said to just go in. She must be a very trusting person," Kellie murmured.

"Even so, she'll have had cameras installed, as well as an electronic lock." He reached past her and opened the door. They stepped right into an office with a desk and several leather chairs placed in front of it. At a glance he saw shelves with family photos, grandchildren. On one wall was a large oil painting of flowers.

As he closed the door, he heard the click. A few moments later a connecting door into the house opened. A small, attractive woman with streaks of silver in her black hair, worn in a bun, entered the room. She looked on the frail side.

"Thank you for being on time. I'm Olympia. Please call me that. You must be Kellie."

"Yes. It's very nice to meet you. Thank you for making time for us so quickly. I'd like to introduce you to my husband, Leandros."

"How do you do." They all shook hands. "Please sit down."

While the therapist took her seat in a comfortable padded chair behind the desk, Leandros helped Kellie. With her hair falling like spun gold to her shoulders from a side part, she looked particularly stunning. She was wearing an aquamarine, two-piece summer suit with short sleeves he hadn't seen before. He loved the color on her.

"We'll discuss the fee after I've decided I can help you. As I told you on the phone, I only counsel you as a couple, not individually."

"You mean you never have private sessions with your clients?" Kellie asked.

"Never, and I never record conversations. Once you start down that road, it doesn't work. To remove suspicion, everything must be said in front of each other in my hearing. Otherwise we're wasting each other's time."

Kellie's face crumpled. He wasn't too thrilled about the rules himself. This counselor drove a hard bargain, reminding him of his own business practices. But in all honesty it made the most sense, and his regard for the older woman went up several notches.

Olympia put on her bifocals. "How long have you been married?"

Leandros decided to let Kellie do the talking.

"Two years and one month."

"Which one of you felt the need for counseling?"

"I did," his wife answered.

"What matters is that you're both here. I'll go out of the room for a few minutes. If you're in agreement with my method, then let me know when I come back in, and we'll get started." She disappeared, leaving them alone. His wife sat there, hunched over.

"What do you think, Kellie?"

Slowly she lifted her head and glanced at him with mournful eyes. "She's the most direct woman I ever met. I think this could be very painful."

He inhaled sharply. "More painful than what we've already been through?"

"Yes," she said without hesitation.

He'd had to ask the question, even though he'd known what her answer would be. Yet upon hearing it, he felt as if she'd just delivered a crippling blow to his midsection. Their problems were like the tip of an iceberg, with nine-tenths lying beneath the surface of the water. Without therapy, they'd be left unexplored, and the prognosis for a happy marriage was anything but good.

Unfortunately, he knew that once they got into deep therapy, the things they found out about each other could bring more pain. It would be a treacherous journey, but they had to make it if they hoped for a resolution that would preserve their marriage. No matter what he'd be forced to go through, he'd do it if he could have back the adorable woman he'd married.

"I want to do it, Kellie."

Her brown eyes swam with tears. "If you really mean it."

His temper flared, but he fought to control it. "I wouldn't have said so otherwise."

Olympia came back into the room. This time Leandros spoke first. "We'd like to go ahead with the therapy. Since we're expecting twins next March, any fee you charge will be worth it if we can fix what's wrong."

Her dark eyes studied them without revealing her thoughts. "That's courageous on both your parts." She took her place at the desk and named her fee. "I'd prefer to see you twice a week for the first month. The sessions will last an hour. When the month is out, it might not be necessary to see you more than once a month or even at all. My only opening left is at eleven in the mornings, Tuesdays and Thursdays."

Leandros didn't need to confer with Kellie. They both wanted the same thing. "We'll be here."

"Good. Then let's get started." The older woman sat back in her chair with her palms pressed together in front of her. "We'll begin with you, Kellie. Why did you marry your husband?"

Bands constricted his lungs while Leandros waited for her answer.

Kellie wouldn't look at him. "Because I fell painfully in love with him."

"Why painfully?"

"Because I didn't want to love a man who'd been married before, let alone one who'd been madly in love. Her name was Petra. Everyone told me they had the perfect marriage."

Leandros stifled a groan. She couldn't have been more wrong.

"Who's everyone?"

"All the people I met before our wedding. His family and friends. I was terrified I would never measure up to the woman who'd died."

"Why would you want to do that? He married *you*."

Kellie looked confounded. "I—I don't know," she stammered.

"Think about that and we'll discuss it at one of your next sessions. For the moment I'd like to know if you had been in love before you met your husband."

"Not like that. Never like that," she whispered.

Her fervency thrilled Leandros.

"But there was someone else?"

"Yes. One of my college friends had wealthy parents who belonged to a club where there was a tennis pro named Rod Silvers. Since I'd played tennis since my junior high days, she often invited me to play with her. That's where I met Rod, and we started dating.

"He was from a prominent Philadelphia family. I was attracted and flattered. But after a month of seeing each other pretty constantly, he stopped calling me. When I broke down and told my friend, she said his family already had someone from the Philadelphia society register picked out for him to marry."

Kellie had mentioned she'd once dated a tennis pro, but this was the first Leandros knew about his background.

"I see," Mrs. Lasko said. "Now I'd like hear when you first suspected all was not well in your marriage."

A few seconds passed before Kellie said, "At our wedding."

"Our *wedding*?" Leandros blurted. Her quiet response stunned him, because he'd noticed a difference in her after they'd gone to his villa to begin their honeymoon. But he'd never suspected she thought anything was wrong.

"I can see this has surprised your husband, Kellie."

Olympia possessed an unflappable demeanor that reminded him of his maternal grandmother. While his heart thundered in his chest from his wife's revelation, the woman went on talking to Kellie with a calm he could only envy.

"How long did you know him before you were married?"

"Three months."

"Was there an official period of engagement?"

"No."

"What happened at the wedding?"

"That's when I became aware I had competition for my husband's affection."

"You mean besides the memory of his dead wife."

"Yes."

"Did it come from another man? Or was it a woman?"

Leandros shot out of the chair, infuriated by the question. "Neither!"

Olympia glanced at him. "That sounded final. Did you hear him, Kellie?"

"Yes," she answered in a muffled voice.

"Go on."

He sat down again, feeling like a ten-year-old child who'd acted out in class and had just been dismissed by his teacher.

"It was a woman."

"Someone he'd known before he met you?"

"Yes."

"Her name is Karmela Paulos," Leandros broke in, completely frustrated because he'd known Kellie would bring her up. "She's the sister of my deceased wife, Petra."

"Karmela is very beautiful and resembles Petra," Kellie continued. "She's smart like her, too. They were only a year apart."

"What did she do that threatened you?"

Upset and curious to hear what Kellie would tell Olympia, Leandros extended his long legs and folded his arms to hold himself in check while he waited for the answer.

"After our wedding at the church on Andros, his family held a reception at their nearby villa. Everyone invited came up to congratulate us. When Karmela appeared with her family, she cupped his face in her hands and gave him a long kiss on the lips. As her eyes slid to mine, I saw an angry flash no woman could mistake for anything other than pure jealousy."

Leandros sat there, stunned. He'd been so excited to make Kellie his wife, he didn't remember that moment. In fact, the events of the reception were a big blur.

"After kissing my husband, she kissed me on the cheek and murmured, 'Good luck in holding on to him.'"

He straightened in the chair, aghast by what he'd just heard. Karmela's childish, petulant behavior was out of bounds at times, but he hadn't known she'd subjected Kellie to it as early as their wedding reception.

"My best friend, Fran, was standing a little distance off. When she came over to congratulate us, she whispered that she'd noticed Karmela had fixated on my husband throughout the day. In her words, 'By no stretch of the imagination could that kiss be construed as platonic.'"

While Leandros was still digesting information that stuck in his throat, Kellie said, "My friend isn't the kind of person who looks for trouble or thinks the worst of anyone. Her opinion wasn't the only one I heard that night on the subject of Karmela."

He furrowed his brows, wondering what else in blazes she was about to reveal that he knew nothing about.

"At the wedding, my husband's best man, Frato, took me aside to congratulate me. He happens to be his first cousin and is very close to him. After he kissed my cheek, he said that he had something to tell me in confidence, but didn't want it getting back to Leandros."

What in the hell?

"Frato confided he was worried about me because Karmela had had a thing for Leandros even before her sister's marriage to him. After the plane crash that killed Petra and their unborn baby, Karmela confided to him that she planned to be the next Mrs. Petralia and give him the child he wanted so desperately."

What?

"Frato said that since I'd beaten Karmela to the altar, he wanted to warn me to watch out for her, because she didn't care who she hurt. He was afraid Leandros had a blind spot when it came to Karmela, so I had my work cut out."

Leandros's blood pressure spiked through the ceiling.

"I could smell alcohol on Frato's breath and feared he'd had too much to drink, but on the heels of Karmela's kiss and my friend's observations, I couldn't completely ignore what he'd told me. Especially when I found out that the Paulos family were neighbors of the Petralia family on Andros and the children had grown up together. But considering it was my first day of marriage, I chose to push it all to the back of my mind."

Incredulous over what he'd heard, Leandros clenched his hands into fists. He couldn't sit here much longer without exploding. The news about Frato had knocked him sideways.

"Why did you keep your husband in the dark about this?"

"B-because I was trying to be the kind of wife who trusted my new husband completely. Since it was his good friend and cousin who'd asked me not to say anything, I just couldn't betray his confidence. But a little over two months ago, Leandros brought Karmela into his office to be one his secretaries."

That hadn't been Leandros's doing, but he wanted to hear the rest before he interrupted her again.

"For my husband to do that meant he'd had talks with Karmela I didn't know about."

You're wrong, Kellie. So wrong I'm sickened by what I'm hearing.

"That's when I feared what Frato had told me was coming true. In response to the news, I asked Leandros if he'd let me come to work at his office, find me a position."

Good grief. That's why she'd asked him for a job? The pain in her voice stung him.

"What did you hope to accomplish?"

"In case Karmela was still infatuated with my husband, I wanted to be closer to him, so he wouldn't turn to her. With hindsight I can see it was very childish of me. When I broached the subject of my being at the office, Leandros dismissed the idea. Naturally I thought the reason he wouldn't want me there is because it would interfere with his interactions with Karmela."

Leandros flew out of his chair a second time, hot with rage over these new revelations about Karmela's behavior. "I told you why I didn't want you at work, Kellie. I preferred to get business and everything associated with it out of the way, so I could come home to my loving wife every night."

Kellie gave him a pained look, reminding him that their relationship had deteriorated severely over those last months. "I told him I wanted a divorce," she went on, talking to Olympia. "The night before I was going to leave for the States, Karmela walked into our apartment from the private elevator, *unannounced*, to bring Leandros some papers."

Just as she'd done the night before last!

"The two of them disappeared into his den for a little while. After she left, I asked him if he needed further proof of her infatuation with him. He denied any knowledge of expecting her, and swore he had no feelings for her. But I'm afraid I couldn't believe him this time, not when he hadn't even deleted her code from the elevator entrance."

Leandros was afraid he'd jump out of his skin. "Once you and I were married, I never gave the code a thought, Kellie. Only the night Karmela let herself in did I remember. You have to believe she came uninvited." He could have strangled his sister-in-law that night. As for the other night…

"None of it matters anymore, Leandros. All I knew was that I had to get out of our marriage."

"All right," Olympia stated. "I've heard enough to understand where suspicions of infidelity, whether warranted or not, put a pall over your marriage from day one. Let's turn to you, Leandros." She eyed him directly. "Why don't you sit down and try to relax."

Relax being the operative word.

Wild with fury over Karmela's behavior, he raked a hand through his hair before doing her bidding.

"If I understand correctly, you and your first wife knew each other for years prior to your marriage."

The change of subject threw him off for a minute. "Yes, but I went out with various girl-friends and had no romantic interest in Petra.

Not until she was living in an apartment in Athens with her sister, who worked for an accounting firm. Both sets of parents asked me to look in on them as a favor, which I did from time to time.

"Petra was an excellent businesswoman who was hired by a local textile company. I admired her drive and intelligence. One thing led to another."

"Did you have an official engagement?"

"Yes. Six months. We were married a year and a half when she was killed."

"You were a widower how long?"

"Two years before I met Kellie."

"Considering you knew your first wife for years and went through a six-month engagement period, your second marriage happened fast. Twelve small weeks, in fact." Olympia scrutinized him. "Why did you ask her to marry you?"

His gaze swerved to his wife. Her wan countenance put him in fresh turmoil. "She thrilled me from the first moment I met her. With the fire lit, that feeling only grew stronger, and I knew I couldn't let her go back to Pennsylvania."

"Tell me, Leandros. When did *you* first know your marriage to Kellie was in trouble?"

Letting out a sigh of frustration, he clasped his hands between his knees. "On our wedding night." His admission brought Kellie's head around in surprise. "When I took her back to the villa, she went through all the motions of being in love with me, but something had changed. I felt she was holding back from me emotionally somehow, and I couldn't figure it out."

He glanced at Kellie. "Now I know why, but at the time I thought it was because she hadn't been married before and everything was still new. I believed that by the time morning came, she'd be the Kellie I'd fallen in love with, but that woman didn't emerge. She was sweet and affectionate as always, but the passion I'd felt from her before the marriage wasn't the same.

"To make things even more complicated, she came down with a rash and hives so severe on the second day of our honeymoon, we had to go to the doctor. We learned she had an allergy to me. Since that meant using protection all the time, it made it impossible for us to get pregnant by normal means."

"How did that make you feel?"

"I won't pretend. It was hard for both of us to hear. We spent the rest of our honeymoon discussing options, and decided we'd try artificial insemination. After the first procedure was done, I took her traveling with me while I looked for new properties. I loved being with her.

"In the beginning, we went everywhere together and spent the odd weekend on Andros. But over the last eight months, she preferred to stay at the apartment in Athens if we weren't going out of town. I assumed maybe she was worrying too much, and wanted to stay close to her doctor. When I asked her about it, she told me nothing was wrong. I could tell she didn't want to discuss it, but I knew the stress of waiting to see if we were pregnant seemed to overtake our lives.

"Two months ago I asked her to go to Rhodes with me. She told me no, that she wanted a separation."

Kellie jerked around, white faced, to look at him. "At the family dinner party a few nights before, Dionne mentioned that Karmela would be accompanying you there on business."

"Then my cousin lied to you, Kellie! I would never take Karmela with me anywhere under any circumstances."

"Why would Dionne do that?"

Leandros studied her pinched features. "I don't know, but I'm going to find out."

Olympia sat forward. "Let's leave the subject of your cousins and sister-in-law for our session on Thursday. Did you go to Rhodes without your wife?"

"I had no choice, because of business arrangements that couldn't be changed. Then unbeknownst to me, I found out she'd made plans for her best friend, Fran, to come to Greece."

"Best friend, as in Frato has been *your* best friend?"

"Yes." Kellie spoke up before he could. "She's been like the sister I never had."

A grimace marred his features. "They were going to take a two-week trip together while I was away on business. After making that announcement, she moved to the guest bedroom. It meant we'd be missing our next appointment with the doctor."

"Since our marriage had failed, I couldn't see the point."

Olympia eyed the two of them. "Artificial insemination is an arduous process even when a couple is totally committed."

"I was prepared to do anything to have a baby," Kellie cried softly.

"No more than I." And now, miracle of miracles, they were expecting twins just before their divorce.

Kellie glanced at him briefly, then turned away. He drew in a fortifying breath. "Even though things were bad between us, when I flew Kellie back to Philadelphia, I told her I didn't want a divorce. That's when she challenged me to go to counseling with her.

"In my anger and bewilderment, I told her I didn't believe in it, and I returned to Athens. But after our separation, I realized I couldn't bear to lose her, so I agreed to it."

"Did you fly back to Pennsylvania to tell her that in person?"

"I didn't have to. She flew here two days ago with the news that she was pregnant. That's when I told her I'd been doing research to find some good therapists here in Athens. If she didn't want to get therapy here, then we'd do it in Philadelphia. After thinking about it, she chose you to help us because of your long record."

That brought the first sign of mirth from Olympia. "I'm an old fossil, all right. When did the subject of getting pregnant first come up?"

"Before we married, I told her I'd love to

have children with her. She told me she couldn't wait to have a baby. Unless I'm wrong, it was a mutual decision before we took our vows."

"You aren't wrong," Kellie blurted in a wounded voice.

Olympia's gaze fell on both of them. "I'd say on that score you've communicated brilliantly. Artificial insemination is not an easy route to go, but you did it—otherwise you wouldn't be expecting twins in the near future. As for the rest, you can see you're poles apart for a married couple who hope to stay together.

"Surely today's revelations have given you your first inkling of where to dig to start finding understanding. You'll have to be brutally honest, open up and listen to each other. You'll be forced to wade through perceptions, whether false or accurate, and no matter how painful, arrive at the truth. I'll see you on Thursday."

Kellie nodded, filling him with relief that she was in agreement. He'd been afraid that when they got out to the car, she would tell him she'd changed her mind, and would refuse to go through with this after all.

While his mind was on the conversation he intended to have with Frato, whether his cousin wanted it or not, Leandros watched Olympia get up from her desk and enter her house through the connecting door. Kellie beat him to the outside door and hurried out to the car, strapping herself in.

He got behind the wheel and backed out to the street. A disturbing silence enveloped them. After heading for the main artery, he turned to her, anxious to fill the rest of their day with something constructive. "Where would you like to go for lunch? Or would you rather eat back at the hotel?"

"The hotel, if that's all right with you."

"Of course. You can rest there for a while."

She recrossed her shapely legs, a sign she was agitated. "Please don't assume I'm always tired."

"I'm sorry."

A heavy sigh escaped her lips. "Forgive me for being cranky."

"After that session, neither of us is at our best." He put on his sunglasses. "You're restless, Kellie. Instead of keeping it all inside until you reach the breaking point, let's take Olympia's advice and start really talking to each other."

"I—I'm afraid...." Her voice faltered.

"Of me?" he demanded.

"Yes—no—I don't know."

"Try me. I swear I won't erupt like I did in her office."

After a long pause, Kellie said, "I have a lot of questions. For one, I don't understand why you sold the penthouse."

Olympia's words still rang in his ears. *Surely today has given you your first inkling of where to dig to start finding understanding. You'll have to be brutally honest, open up and listen to each other. You'll be forced to wade through perceptions, whether false or accurate, and no matter how painful, to arrive at the truth.*

He cast his wife a covert glance before throwing the truth at her. "Pure and simple, I couldn't stand living there without you. That was the only reason. When I got back from Pennsylvania and walked into the living room, it hit me you wouldn't be coming home again. I couldn't take it, and phoned Frato. He'd coveted the penthouse and had said as much many times."

Through the gold curtain of hair, her lovely profile was partially visible, yet her expression hidden. "But I know you missed Petra horribly after she died. Why didn't you sell it then?"

If they hadn't been in therapy today, Leandros could see Kellie would never have had the temerity to ask that question. Now that she had, she deserved all the honesty he could give her.

"As you know, I'd rather live on Andros, and would have always lived there and commuted. But Petra wanted to live in Athens, and kept looking for a place for us. She met with a Realtor who knew the penthouse and its furnishings were up for sale if someone could pay the right price for it. She fell in love with it and wanted nothing else.

"To be honest, I didn't want to move in there, but I bought it to please her. Only two things about it appealed to me. The private elevator and the helicopter landing pad. I figured I could wing back to Andros without fuss when I wanted, but the penthouse never felt like home.

"Petra was a working woman who traveled a lot and kept late hours, like me. She wasn't there that much and hated to cook. That's because she threw all her creativity into her job. We ate out ninety percent of the time. When we entertained, she had the food catered. Once we found out she was expecting, it didn't stop her from working. When the plane went down, she'd been returning from a business trip."

"How awful that period was for you." Kellie's voice shook.

"It was, but you need to understand she never turned the apartment into a haven. *You're* the one who did that for us. Every day I found myself watching the clock, waiting to get home to you and make love. Half the time I cut my work short so we could have more time together in the evenings.

"Without you there, the memories tortured me. You know how it was with us. When I traveled, I had to have you with me—otherwise I couldn't have stood the separations. When you stopped going with me, it was torture."

She'd gone stone-cold quiet.

"Are you upset I sold it?"

He heard a sharp intake of breath. "If you'd asked me that question before we got married, I would have told you I was overjoyed."

CHAPTER FOUR

"WHAT?" LEANDROS'S THOUGHTS reeled, trying to keep up with Kellie.

"Since I'd never been married before, I wanted to start out our life together without memories of Petra. In my mind, that penthouse was her home with you. On our honeymoon, when you told me you had a special wedding present for me, I assumed you were selling it and had plans to find a place in Athens for the two of us.

"Truthfully, I never liked the penthouse. I guess I wanted a real home on the ground, one you and I picked out together."

Leandros groaned. "That small sailboat I bought you hardly qualified, did it?"

"I *love* that boat. It's been one of my great joys."

His hand tightened on the steering wheel. "Why in heaven's name didn't you tell me you didn't want to live at the penthouse?"

"And have you think I was a scheming woman who married you for your money and was already rearranging your life and your assets?" she cried out.

Her reaction astonished him. "Where's all this coming from, Kellie?"

"It doesn't matter now."

"The hell it doesn't. Tell me!"

She smoothed some golden strands away from her temple. "When I resigned from my job at the advertising agency, my boss, Brandon Howard, said, 'Now that you're marrying a man as rich as Croesus, you'll be able to buy anything you want, and become the paparazzo's favorite target.

"But if you think you're the only woman in his life, because of all the toys the great Leandros Petralia gives you, you're even more naive than I thought. Have you ever known a wealthy Greek playboy to be faithful to one woman all his life? You can't name one! It's a fairy tale, Kellie. Wake up and get out of it before it's too late.'"

A gush of adrenaline attacked Leandros's body. "Now I'm beginning to understand some of your initial concerns about Fran getting involved with Nik. It's all making sense. But don't you know that was your employer's jealousy talking, because you would never go out with him?"

"I realize that now, but at the time he made it sound so ugly, I determined never to be the creature he was talking about. No matter how much I might have wanted to ask you to sell your penthouse for my sake, it wasn't something I could have found the nerve to do.

"It would have given your family and friends more ammunition to find fault with me, and start saying that I was trying to change you to get more gifts out of you."

"My family loves you!"

"In your eyes, Leandros, because you see what you want to see. But I heard your cousins Dionne and Zera talking with Karmela at your grandmother's birthday six months after we were married. They didn't know I'd picked up enough Greek to understand what they were saying. It was quite illuminating to learn all the ways I didn't come close to matching Petra's virtues.

"They saw a foreigner who would never fit in, who couldn't speak Greek in the beginning or get pregnant, who put you through one artificial insemination procedure after another."

"But you never heard my parents say such a thing!"

"That's true," she admitted quietly. "I'm sorry. Your parents are wonderful."

"They love you, Kellie. Just remember that Dionne and Zera are close friends with Karmela. That would explain the damaging conversation." His gut twisted. "You should have told me. You've suffered in silence all this time."

"I married you, not them, Leandros. Families will gossip. That I understand and forgive."

"Your generous nature should make them ashamed."

"I wish I hadn't said anything. As for the penthouse, I would hardly call living there a penance."

"But it took an emotional toll," he muttered grimly. Everything had taken a toll....

By this time they'd arrived at the hotel. He drove into his underground parking space and helped her out of the car to the elevator. After they'd reached his suite, he asked her what she'd like to eat, and called for room service. But when they sat down at the table to eat, he wasn't hungry.

"Kellie? Would you answer me something honestly?"

"What else do we have if we don't have that?"

He leaned forward. "The last thing you said to me before I left Philadelphia was that I shouldn't have married you, because you weren't good enough for me. I never understood where that came from until today, when you told Olympia about Rod's background. For you to clump his family with mine is—"

"His rejection made me feel inferior," she interrupted. "It hurt my pride, nothing more."

"Maybe that feeling was linked to Petra," he theorized. "Why didn't you talk to me about it?"

"I suppose I didn't want to bring her up if it would be painful for you. I realize now that isn't the case. I shouldn't have said I wasn't good enough for you. It was a foolish remark. You and your family are nothing like that. In my pain I've said a lot of things I regret."

"That works both ways. I should never have shut you down when you asked if I'd go to counseling with you."

For the next few minutes they ate in silence.

"I have another confession to make, Leandros."

He put down his coffee cup.

"When you wanted to keep trying the procedure—even though we weren't getting along—I couldn't believe you weren't discouraged," Kellie murmured. "I'm afraid I started thinking that the only reason you married me was to replace the child you'd lost."

He eyed her soulfully. "If that were true, I would have suggested we adopt a baby and save ourselves all the angst we went through. But I loved you and knew how much *you* wanted the experience of being pregnant. I'd already been through that part with Petra."

"I know," she whispered, "and I was secretly envious of her. Years ago, when Fran told me she could never have a baby, I felt terrible for her, but I didn't begin to understand the depth of her pain until the doctor explained how hard you and I would have to work to conceive. You just take it for granted that you'll grow up, get married and have a baby. But it doesn't always play out like that."

"I'll admit I wasn't prepared to find out you were allergic to me. If you want to know the truth, I thought your hives were a physical manifestation that you'd regretted marrying me."

Her eyes teared. "You're kidding me."

"No. Not at all. My heart almost failed me to think the woman I'd married was no longer enamored in the same way. It hurt *my* pride. I know there were times when we couldn't communicate because I couldn't handle it. That didn't help us at a time when we needed to be totally supportive and confident of our love."

"Oh, Leandros...I had no idea."

He took a steadying breath. "This morning's session has opened my eyes to many things, not the least of which is the part Frato has played in our lives. Before we do anything else, I want to sit down with him in person."

Kellie rested her fork on the salad plate. "Because you don't believe I told the truth about him?"

Leandros's hurt and anger were simmering beneath the surface. "I believe you, Kellie. What I didn't know until a few hours ago was that he's not the friend I thought he was. Apparently blood *isn't* thicker than water."

Her brown eyes filled with more pain. "Don't say that, Leandros. He's your cousin, and was only trying to put me in the picture."

Leandros wiped the corner of his mouth with the napkin. "I'll reserve judgment until we've talked to him."

"We?"

"Yes. We're going to take a leaf out of Olympia's book and face him together, where there's no squirming room. He'll be at the office. I'm going to call him now and tell him to meet us at the villa on Andros after he's through work today. I'll put it in terms that won't allow him to avoid the summons."

She pushed herself away from the table. "Well, if you're going to do that, I'm going to phone Fran. She's left several messages over the last few days and has no idea I'm in Athens. I need to respond. Excuse me."

Encouraged that, since their therapy session, they weren't at each other's throats, and she felt like talking to Fran, Leandros pulled out his cell to call his cousin on his private line. Frato answered on the third ring.

"Hey, Leandros—missing the job already?" he teased.

His affection for Frato made this difficult for him. "Actually, something of vital importance has come up. No matter what you've got planned for this evening, I need to talk to you in private and want you to fly out to Andros. How soon can I expect you?"

After a period of quiet his cousin said, "This sounds serious."

"Make no mistake. It is."

"I'm in Volos, doing a walk-through of the construction for the new resort. Those specs you worked up really helped. I should be finished by two-thirty at the latest, then I'll fly straight to Andros."

"I'll be waiting."

"Leandros? What's wrong?"

"I can't talk now. See you later." He purposely hung up, for fear his anger would overtake any good judgment or magnanimity he had left.

Next he phoned Stefon and told him to get the helicopter ready.

"Kellie? I'm so thrilled it's you! I told Nik that if I didn't hear from you soon, I was going to call your aunt."

"Sorry I didn't get back to you before now, but a lot has been going on. Is this a bad time?" She sank onto the edge of the bed in the guest bedroom to talk.

"Not at all. I just put Demi down for her nap. The next time you see her, you won't believe how much she has grown. I sent you pictures, but you have to see her in person. She's so sweet and beautiful, Kellie. Gorgeous like Nik. I love them both so much I can hardly stand it, but forgive me for rattling on."

The happiness in her voice caused Kellie's eyes to fill with tears. "That's the kind of news I long to hear. After warning you against Nik, I feel so terrible."

"You're my best friend. Don't you know I understood why? Please promise me you won't bring it up again. It's all in the past. So how soon do you take possession of the house in Parkwood? We're going to fly over and help you and your aunt and uncle move in."

"I love you for offering, but I've had to put my plans for the house on hold." In fact, she needed to call her Realtor after she hung up with Fran.

"Why? Was there a snag in the negotiations?"

"N-no," she stammered.

"Kellie…I can tell by that hesitant sound in your voice something's wrong. What is it?"

"Are you sitting down?"

"Do I need to?" she cried in alarm.

"No. I'm sorry. It's good news."

"Thank heaven."

"This week I found out I'm seven weeks pregnant with twins."

"Twins?" Fran squealed with joy.

"Can you believe it?" Kellie half laughed through the tears. "After all my angst?"

"It's another miracle! Oh, wait till I tell Nik! How are you feeling?"

"Dr. Creer gave me medicine for the nausea. I'm doing fine."

"Forgive me for the next question, but I have to ask. How soon are you going to tell Leandros? I have to say, he's so devastated by what's happened, I hardly recognize him."

Kellie had hardly recognized him at the office. She'd been waiting for Fran's question. "He already knows. I flew here day before yesterday."

Another cry came over the phone line, almost bursting her eardrum. "You're in Athens?"

"Yes. There's so much to tell you, I hardly know where to start. Unfortunately, I can't stay on the phone right now because we're flying to Andros the minute I get off. But I promise I'll call you tomorrow. Maybe we can meet for a late lunch on Thursday. Leandros and I will be back in town for the next session with our marriage counselor."

She heard another gasp. "Leandros Petralia, *the* Leandros Petralia, finally agreed to go to counseling?"

"Yes. I flew to Athens to tell him I was pregnant. That's when he told me he wants another chance to save our marriage. I don't know if it will work, but I'll tell you all about it tomorrow. Give that baby and Nik a big kiss from me. *Au revoir*, for now," she said. It was a habit she'd picked up since their boarding school days in France. Aware Leandros would be waiting for her, she clicked off before Fran could say anything else.

After leaving a message for her Realtor to call her back, Kellie freshened up. But before she joined her husband, she ran her hands over her stomach.

"My precious little babies," she whispered. "You deserve a mother and father who love each other desperately and have no secrets."

She might have known Leandros would insist on talking to his cousin ASAP. It was his way to swoop in and take care of whatever needed doing, but this wasn't a business transaction. They would need to tread carefully to find common ground, in order to deal with their problems. Today was a start, but what if this didn't work?

Kellie put her head back. Refusing to think negative thoughts at this early stage, she walked through to the sitting room. He'd changed out of his suit into jeans and a burgundy polo shirt. She averted her eyes to keep from staring at his well-defined physique.

Kellie had always been wildly attracted to

him, but in the end even such a strong attraction hadn't been able to overcome her distrust and pain. She could scarcely credit that he was willing to go to counseling with her. However, she needed to remember this was only the first day of therapy. A frisson of fear ran through her because she knew anything could go wrong in the weeks ahead.

"Were you able to reach Frato?"

His haunted gray eyes swerved to hers. "He'll be arriving later this afternoon. How's Fran?"

"She sounds happier than I've ever known her to be."

"Did you tell her about the twins?"

"Yes. She's elated for us. I told her I'd see her on Thursday after our therapy session."

"Good." Leandros's gaze swept over Kellie. "Is there anything you'd like to do before we leave for Andros?"

"No."

"Then let's go."

Except for the kiss at his office, they'd had no contact or relations in over two months. He didn't try to touch her again except to help her get in and out of the car or the helicopter. In those early months, they'd never been able to stay out of each other's arms. Even though

Leandros had admitted in therapy he'd felt a change in her since the wedding, he seemed to have brushed his fears to the back of his mind, with the result that she was convinced he thought all was well.

Somehow she needed to learn how to shut off her memories of what it used to be like with them. Otherwise she wouldn't be able to get through this experiment. But it was so hard when they slept under the same roof at night. He went to his room, she went to hers, where she died a little each time without him.

Once more Kellie had to fight the desire that shot through her when he grasped her arm to assist her into the helicopter. His touch always played havoc with her senses. Christos couldn't help but notice.

With her heart still pounding, they were carried over the Parthenon of the three-thousand-year-old city to the island where she'd known joy, accompanied by doubts and fears she'd never been able to shake.

Now she was facing a new fear. She'd seen the wintry look in Leandros's eyes when she'd told him what Frato had said to her at the wedding. Her husband was a wonderful man, but when crossed he made an even more wonderful adversary. Kellie had it in her heart to feel sorry for Frato, who had no idea what was waiting for him.

It wounded her that there might be trouble between the cousins, who'd always been so close. That was one of the reasons she'd never told Leandros anything. But therapy had forced her to open up if they hoped to save their marriage. It was too late to beg her husband to call off this meeting. In any case, she didn't want to.

For Leandros to hear from his cousin's lips that he had a blind spot where Karmela was concerned would give credence to what she'd told him. Her husband would have to take her fears seriously. She was so deep in thought, she didn't realize they'd landed until Leandros called to her.

"Kellie?" He looked worried. "Are you all right?"

"Yes. Of course." She unstrapped herself and got out of the helicopter with his help. This time she felt his hand slide down her arm like a caress, as if reluctant to let her go. Her breath caught before she moved away to thank Stefon for another safe flight.

Leandros was right behind her as she hurried down the path to his villa. With each step she wondered how many times he and his first wife had rushed into his house to be alone and shut out the world.

When Kellie reached the door, she waited for him to unlock it, but he stood there instead, staring at her with penetrating eyes. "After the many revelations during our therapy session, I realize you have more questions about Petra and me. I wish you'd asked me long ago. I would have told you anything."

He seemed to be reading her mind. "I should have, but I wanted to pretend you didn't have a past. That was another mistake on my part."

"Kellie," he said in a tone of exasperation. "Let's not talk about the mistakes we made. Before we go inside, I want you to know something important."

She gripped her handbag a little tighter.

"Petra agreed to our wedding taking place at the church in Stenies, but after the ceremony, we spent the night aboard her father's yacht with all the amenities. It's moored in a bay two miles from here. The next day we flew to New York for our honeymoon."

Kellie couldn't believe they'd chosen New York when they could have stayed here.

"She was never happy on Andros. It was too steeped in the past for her. She craved life in the big city. We rarely spent time here. On the few times we did come, it was to see her parents. At her insistence, we always spent the night at her parents' villa."

"But what about *your* wishes?"

"I came home when she was away overnight on business." Leandros searched Kellie's eyes. "I'm telling you all this to let you know we never slept in my villa. No woman has ever stayed overnight here except you."

While that piece of news sank in, he turned and unlocked the door. After opening it, he suddenly picked her up like a bride. "I want to carry you over the threshold again. This time you can have the sure knowledge that every memory inside these walls since we met is associated with you and no one else."

She didn't doubt he was telling her the truth. His sincerity reached that vulnerable spot inside her.

"Leand—" She'd started to say his name, but it got muffled as his hungry mouth came down on hers. He began kissing her with growing urgency, as he'd done on their wedding night. For a moment it was déjà vu. Without effort he swung her around and carried her to his bedroom. Before she knew it they

were tangled in each other's arms on top of the bed, and she found herself clinging helplessly to him.

"I love you, Kellie. More than you can imagine. Let me love you. I need you, *agapi mou*."

Here she was again, succumbing to her needs and his. Though he'd relieved her of her false assumptions to do with Petra, there was still so much to deal with, she didn't dare let this go any further. She knew herself too well. To allow herself to be blinded by passion and make love with him might satisfy the ache inside her for the moment. But it wouldn't solve the things that were still wrong outside this bed.

When he lifted his head so she could breathe, Kellie took advantage and rolled away. She got to her feet, wobbling horribly. He lay there looking devastated. "Why have you pulled away from me?"

She held on to his dresser for support. "I'm glad you told me about Petra. It has helped a lot. I *do* love you, Leandros. That will never change, but—"

"But Karmela is still the big impediment." His eyes flashed a gunmetal-gray as he got off the bed.

Kellie took a deep breath. "It isn't just Karmela. I think that until we've finished with therapy, we should concentrate on our problems and not sleep together. I can't forget that Frato will be here in a little while, and I have to admit I'm frightened."

"Why?" he demanded. "Because you haven't told me the truth? Or is it because you finally divulged a secret he asked you not to tell me, and you fear repercussions?"

She clasped her hands together. "I would never lie to you. I'm just afraid of what it might do to your friendship after he's confronted. A rift between the two of you could hurt your family in ways that make me ill to contemplate."

"Because you're afraid they'll blame you?"

"Deep down I suppose I am."

Leandros's eyes glittered in pain. "No rift could be more deadly than the one between you and me. I'll go to any lengths to fix it." She believed him—otherwise he wouldn't be going to therapy with her. "If it alienates my cousin and me, or my family, so be it. I'm going down to the beach for a swim. Do you want to come with me?"

"Yes," she said, making a snap decision that seemed to surprise him. "I'll go in the other bedroom and change into my suit."

Over the past few months, before she'd gone back to Philadelphia, he'd become used to her turning him down. But as Olympia had pointed out, there was a lot Kellie had kept from Leandros. She realized now she'd done so out of fear. Unfortunately, it had combined with his hurt pride to help contribute to the serious problems in their marriage. His determination to put it back together at any cost made her cognizant that she needed to play an equal part in this.

Throwing a wrap over the white bikini he'd given her on her twenty-eighth birthday, four months ago, she joined him at the front door and they walked down the steps to the beach.

"Ooh, this sand is almost hot."

Leandros eyed her up and down after she removed her wrap. His gaze focused on her stomach, which was getting thicker, but so far wasn't protruding. "Then let's get you in the water quick."

"Oh no, you don't!" she cried, and started running toward it, barely escaping his arms, which would have picked up her again. Kellie was a good swimmer and took off, not worried about the depth, since it was fairly shallow for about a hundred feet. He came after her like a torpedo and circled her, preventing her from going out any farther.

"You need to be careful now that our little unborn babies are starting to make their presence known."

Kellie treaded water. "You noticed?" she teased, feeling playful in a brand-new way, because therapy had opened up a dialogue, and she no longer felt threatened by Petra's specter.

His white smile turned her heart over. "You're no longer concave. I love your new shape."

"I'll hold you to that when I need to be carted around in a wheelbarrow at seven months." After the words flew out of her mouth, she realized her mistake. They might not be together in seven months, or even in one more month.

He moved closer, catching her around the hips. The next thing she knew he'd turned her body so her back was against his chest. A voluptuous warmth filled her as moved his hands over her stomach, exploring her until her senses leaped. "I've got the world in my arms," he whispered, kissing her on the side of her neck.

Kellie was so filled with chaotic emotions, she couldn't talk.

"When you told me you were expecting twins, you made me the happiest man alive, not only for me, but for you. I'm here for you in every way."

"I'm happy for you, too, Leandros. No man ever tried harder to become a father. You never let me give up. For that you have my undying gratitude." His touch had reduced her to pulp, so she was slow to realize she could hear a helicopter coming close to the estate. "That will be Frato!"

"So it is, but we'll beat him. Let's keep our personal business to ourselves."

"I agree."

Leandros pulled her with him to shore, then picked her up again and carried her up the steps into the villa, without taking an extra breath. "I'll meet the helicopter and walk him down here. That should give you enough time to change."

He lowered a hard kiss to her mouth before he took off out the front door to greet his cousin. She pressed fingers to her lips, which still tingled as she watched him leave.

He wore black swim trunks that rode low on his hips.

He looked magnificent.

CHAPTER FIVE

LEANDROS WANTED A LOT MORE than his wife's gratitude as he approached the pilot's side of the helicopter. He waited until Frato started to climb out before he told Stefon to stay put. "My cousin will be needing a ride back to Athens, but I don't know the time. You go ahead and use the guest cottage. He'll ring you later."

After the pilot nodded, Leandros walked around the other side. Six feet tall, his cousin was still in a business suit. His dark curly hair and brown eyes proclaimed him a Petralia. Leandros's coloring differed because he'd inherited his mother's gray eyes.

"You made good time, Frato. Thanks for dropping everything to get here so fast. As you can see, I was taking a swim."

"Your phone call made me nervous, so I came as soon as I could. I didn't know you were going to vacation at home."

"My plans are subject to change from moment to moment."

Frato stopped walking long enough to look at him. "That sounded cryptic. What's going on?"

"That's what I want to know. But let's go in the house first. You need to get out of this heat and shed your jacket."

"If I didn't know better, I'd think you were setting me up," he said with a nervous laugh.

His cousin was a quick study. "If I didn't know better, I'd think maybe that was a guilty conscience talking," Leandros replied.

Frato stopped at the front door. "You *are* setting me up!"

When it unexpectedly opened, revealing Kellie, his jaw went slack. She'd arranged her damp, golden hair in a loose knot and changed into jeans and a summery, blouson-type top in a delicious shade of ice-blue. Pregnancy had made her radiant. "Hello, Frato." She kissed him on both cheeks. "Come in and let me fix you something cool while Leandros gets dressed."

"You're back!" His cousin more or less staggered into the living room. "I had no idea."

She nodded. "Do you want a fruit drink or something stronger?"

"Nothing for me." He removed his jacket and tossed it over one of the chairs.

"Then please sit down. It's good to see you."

"I'll be right back." Leandros disappeared to get dressed. In under a minute he returned, wearing shorts and a sport shirt he was still buttoning. "You're sure you won't have a drink?"

Frato shook his head. "I know you when you've got something important on your mind. Why don't we just get to the point."

Leandros stood in front of his cousin, who'd taken a seat on one end of the couch. Kellie sat on the other. The moisture on Frato's upper lip wasn't all due to the heat. Leandros detected nervous tension.

"Today I learned of a confidence you shared with Kellie at our wedding. You told her not to tell me. Do you recall what I'm talking about?"

His cousin looked mystified. "I'm afraid I don't. If you say this happened the night of your nuptials, I remember doing more drinking than usual."

"I could smell the alcohol." Kellie spoke up. "You took me aside to congratulate me. Then you told me some things that were very disturbing, before you asked me to keep it to myself. I honored your wishes until this morning, Frato, but I have two regrets. One, that you ever told me anything, and two, that I kept it from Leandros for so long."

"Refresh my memory." Frato could be obstinate when he wanted.

Leandros listened as she repeated verbatim what she'd told Olympia. The room went an unearthly quiet after she'd finished. Frato got a sick look and moved off the couch to gaze out the window with his back toward them.

"Has it all jelled yet?" Leandros asked in a quiet voice.

His cousin continued to say nothing. Leandros moved closer. "So it's true what you told Kellie?"

Frato finally wheeled around with a tormented look in his eyes. "I meant no harm, Leandros. I swear it."

Anger raged inside him. "How would you know if Karmela had feelings for me before I married Petra?"

"Because she told me!" he blurted.

"How intriguing. Why would she tell *you*?"

"Because I've always been crazy about Karmela." That was news to Leandros. "There've been a few things in our lives I haven't told you. Especially after she refused to go out with me.

When I pressed her for a reason, she said she'd been in love with you since she was a teenager on the island."

"Then it was a fantasy of her own infantile imagination."

"Several girls had a crush on you. But unlike them, she never got over it."

After Karmela's performance the other night, Leandros knew it was true. "Then what purpose did you think it would serve to run to my brand-new wife and alarm her?"

Frato's head reared back. "Because you were so oblivious. I was in love with her, but it did no good while she had her heart set on you. When she found out you were marrying Kellie, she told me that one way or another, she was going to get pregnant with your baby. In her mind she assumed that when it happened, you'd have to get a divorce and marry her."

"Surely you could see she was delusional then," Leandros exclaimed. After her appearance at the office, he realized Petra's sister had a problem that had needed a psychiatrist a long time ago. He was appalled at his own lack of vision, but Kellie had seen it. *She'd* been the one hurt by Karmela at the very beginning of their marriage.

"All I saw was a woman who'd had to live in Petra's shadow. I figured that if I bided my time, she would eventually turn to me. But when I saw how she kissed you at the wedding, I couldn't take it and started drinking."

So Frato had noticed that kiss, too. Leandros hadn't remembered anything but his love for Kellie.

His cousin turned to her. "I felt I had to warn you about what was going on. It was because I liked you and was afraid for you."

"Afraid for my wife?" Leandros bit out.

"Yes." He turned back to Leandros. "Karmela always seemed to have you wrapped around her little finger. It looked like she could do no wrong in your eyes. From my vantage point you let her get away with whatever she wanted."

"So you assumed I'd welcome my own sister-in-law into my bed?" Leandros was livid.

Frato's brow rose. "I didn't know, did I?"

"Good grief! What's happened to you? Where's the cousin I grew up with?"

"You got the woman you wanted! Life was easier for you."

Leandros couldn't believe what he was hearing. "I was going to wait to tell Kellie everything until I'd talked to you. But now this can't wait. Though you don't deserve an explanation, I'm going to give you one.

"When Petra and I started seeing each other, she asked me to be kind to her sister. She worried that Karmela would start feeling abandoned and alone after we got married. Now that I have certain information I didn't have two years ago, I'm convinced Petra knew her sister was very disturbed, but she was afraid to tell me.

"As a favor to her, because she was so concerned, I agreed we would let Karmela come and go from the penthouse like she was part of the family. But I never liked it."

Frato gesticulated with his arms. "Then you understand it was an act she put on for Petra, to win her sympathy and get closer to you."

"I agree and I'm convinced." It was all making an ugly kind of sense. "Now I need the answer to another question. If you were so worried I might take advantage of the situation, then perhaps you'd like to tell me and Kellie a couple of things. Why did you beg me to let her come to work under Mrs. Kostas? And why didn't you want anyone to know it was your doing?"

Kellie's shocked cry was music to Leandros's ears. He prayed his wife was taking all this in.

"Because that favor was for *me*," his cousin insisted. "Karmela never left me alone about coming to work for the company, but I wanted it to look aboveboard, and that meant the decision had to come from you."

A scowl broke out on Leandros's face. "I thought you said she wasn't interested in you."

"In the beginning that was true. But I'm not a quitter. It had been a long time since your wedding to Kellie. About eight months ago we started seeing each other and one thing led to another. Since she came to work in your office, things have been really good behind the scenes," he admitted.

"What happened to Anya?"

"I only see her from time to time, but that's all over now."

Leandros wondered if he'd ever really known his cousin.

"I have more news and might as well let you in on it, since it's going to get out pretty soon," Frato continued. "Karmela and I are going to get married."

"You *what*?"

"Shocking to you, isn't it," he muttered. "Don't you know that's why I took you up on your offer and bought the penthouse? In five years I'll have it completely paid off. She loves it there because it feels like home to her."

Kellie's stunned gaze flew to Leandros. By now she'd gotten to her feet. "There's something you need to know before you make a mistake that could ruin your life, Frato," she said.

"What do you mean?"

"The night before Leandros flew me back to Philadelphia, a month ago, Karmela came to the penthouse *uninvited*. You see, she'd heard the gossip about us getting a divorce, and thought I'd already left for the States.

"What she didn't know was that I'd been sick that night and had to go to the E.R. Leandros brought me back to the penthouse. While we were there, Karmela walked in as if she lived there. I could tell she was shocked to see me, but she covered it well and said she'd brought papers from the office for Leandros to look over and sign.

"Did she tell you about that visit? I can give you the exact date and time. Before you marry her, you'd better find out the truth!"

Frato got that bewildered look on his face, one Leandros had seen many times in their childhood. "Since Petra died, I've never given

Karmela permission to come to the penthouse," Leandros told him. "If I were you, I'd ask her about that night. If she can satisfy you that she had a legitimate right to use my private elevator and walk in on me unannounced and unexpected, then it appears you're the one living in an oblivious state."

His cousin got off the couch again and started pacing.

"Frato," Kellie said in a kindly voice. "I'm very sorry, but it's clear to me Karmela has been using you all this time to get to Leandros. That's why she wanted to come to work at his office. She hasn't given up on this fantasy of hers, and needs professional help. If you marry her, you're in for so much pain, you can't imagine."

While his cousin digested everything, Leandros made a decision. "Why don't you stay overnight on the island with your family? If Karmela is expecting you at the penthouse, tell her you had business that kept you longer than planned. Tomorrow you need to call her into the office and tell her you have to let her go."

Frato hung his head. "I can't fire her."

"Then you want me to do it? I'd rather it came from you."

His cousin looked terrified. "I can't. Leandros—if you insist on this, I'll lose her!"

"We don't have a choice here. Though this is going to be painful for you, I have more news. Do you know where she was at eleven two nights ago?"

"Yes. She said she had to work late, and didn't get back to the apartment until midnight."

"She told you a lie, Frato. While I was working at my desk, she came into my office with a tray of food."

"I don't understand."

It was now or never if Leandros was going to get through to him. "I have no idea how long she'd been in the building, but everyone else had gone home at quitting time. I asked her to leave, but she seemed to think it was some sort of game."

"What do you mean?"

"She acted like a rebellious teenager, wanting to know my business. First she cast disparaging remarks about Kellie. Then she pulled tears about how much she knew I missed Petra, and that she wanted to help me. I believe she's ill, as ill as she was at my wedding to Kellie, but I didn't realize it then. She's gotten sicker with time. I came close to removing her physically from my office before she finally left."

His cousin paled. Who would have guessed that Karmela would turn out to be Frato's Achilles' heel?

Kellie shook her head. "She needs to be let go, Frato. If you lose her because of it, then it will prove she was never really yours to lose. Don't you see this is the only way, for the good of the company and our personal lives? How could anyone hope to function with all that subterfuge going on?"

Perspiration broke out on his forehead. "She'll turn her family against ours and everyone will blame me."

Leandros's jaw hardened. "That will be nothing compared to the fact that she's already created enough trouble between Kellie and me to bring us to the brink of divorce!"

"But they're your in-laws! Out of respect for Petra, how can you do that?"

With that remark, Leandros realized his cousin wasn't capable of viewing the situation rationally right now. Maybe never.

"How can I not? You've missed the point, Frato. I have no doubt her parents have been worried about Karmela for years. When this gets out, it's possible they'll be able to find her the help she needs. While they're doing that, you can move on. Don't forget I'm on vacation until further notice and need you to run the company."

Frato reached for his jacket and headed for the door. "I've got to get back to Athens, where I can think."

"It's your life. But if you're tempted to tell Karmela anything before we meet tomorrow, at nine in the morning, then word could get back to the board through her. You'll be lucky if they only give you a forced leave of absence from the company until you come to your senses."

His cousin wasn't listening. No sooner had he disappeared than Leandros's cell phone rang. It was his mother, who explained she'd just returned from town, and saw the helicopter. "I didn't know you were here."

"Frato and I were having a meeting, but he's leaving now."

"Then come up for dinner."

"I can't tonight, *Mana*."

"Leandros…your papa and I hardly see you these days."

"I know, but I'll make it up to you." He wanted Kellie with him when they told his parents about the twins, but they needed to have another session of therapy before he felt they could inform his family of what was happening. "Right now I'm in the middle of delicate negotiations and don't have the time." It was the truth.

"I've been concerned about you. The last time I saw you, you looked too thin. Since Kellie left, you haven't been taking good enough care of yourself."

"Don't worry about me. I'll call you very soon, I promise."

He rang off and went in search of his wife, who'd gone into the kitchen. When he found her, she was eating a peach. He'd like to eat one of those and then start on her, but that was an activity he had to put on hold for the time being.

"How's your mother?"

"Being motherish."

Kellie flashed him a sad smile. "My aunt gets like that, too."

"Let's drive somewhere along the coast for dinner. I'm starving, as well."

"That sounds good. I'll grab my purse."

As they walked out the front door, the helicopter flew overhead, taking Frato back to Athens. Leandros was thankful he'd gone.

Once they got in the car and were on the

road, she turned to him. "Do you think he'll tell Karmela?"

Leandros slanted her a veiled glance. "There was a time when I thought I knew my cousin, but no longer. It's anyone's guess what we'll find when we arrive at the office tomorrow."

She glanced at the shimmering blue water. "I've always liked Frato. It's so sad that he's been enamored of someone who never loved him. My heart aches for him."

"It's possible this intervention will shake the scales from his eyes. I care deeply for my cousin and would like to see him work this out with as few repercussions as possible."

"Do you know one of your great traits is your charitable attitude about people, even under the worst of circumstances?" Her comment warmed him.

They drove in silence another five miles to a fishing village before she spoke her mind. "I—I wish you'd told me it was Frato's idea to bring her into the office…." Kellie's voice faltered. "Why didn't you tell me she walked in on you two nights ago?"

"I could have, but I was waiting to hear what Frato had to say first before I laid every card on the table." Leandros flicked her a glance. "For that matter, I wish you'd told me what he'd said the night of our wedding. As we've both found out, my cousin knows how to wear you down until you end up doing what he wants."

"I—I never wanted to believe you were interested in Karmela," she admitted.

"The idea was so ludicrous, I couldn't understand your suspicions. I was blind in the beginning, because I was so in love with you. But between Fran's and Frato's observations, it's no wonder the bloom was off our wedding night. Frato can be a valuable asset to the company when he's out doing business. But in our case, he's helped the enemy within."

"I remember that quote from Marcus Cicero. 'A nation can survive its fools, and even the ambitious. But it can't survive treason from within.'"

"Exactly. Years ago my father made me memorize it when I started working for the company."

"How does the rest of it go? I'm positive you know it."

He flashed her a smile, because for a few minutes it felt as if they were really communicating again. "'An enemy at the gates is less formidable, for he is known and carries his banner openly. But the traitor moves amongst those within the gate freely. He speaks in accents familiar to his victims, but works secretly in the night to undermine the pillars of the city.'"

After he'd spoken, Leandros felt the shudder that ran through her body even though they weren't touching. "He could have been describing what's happened to us," she murmured

"When you think about it, those words could apply to your former boss, too. Once you told him you were getting married, he couldn't leave it alone and planted doubts in your mind, all in the name of wanting to keep you for himself."

"He never had me." Kellie rested her forehead in her hand. "His assumptions were so hurtful and angered me so much, you'll never know. But looking back, I realize I did worse. In my zeal to protect Fran from getting hurt after her painful divorce, I made a lot of assumptions about Nik that weren't the truth. You have no idea how ashamed I am. He must think I'm horrible." Tears ran down her cheeks.

Leandros pulled into the parking area of one of their favorite seaside restaurants. To his sorrow they hadn't been here for at least six months. He shut off the engine and turned to her. "You're wrong, Kellie." He wiped the moisture from her cheeks with his thumb. "Nik wasn't as completely open as he should have been with Fran about the real reasons he'd never married, thus arousing your suspicions. He regrets that."

She looked away from him. "You're just being diplomatic, but that's another thing about you I admire. I happen to know my aspersions about him hurt you. The breakdown of our marriage turned me into someone I didn't like."

"I didn't like myself, either, Kellie. By the end, I was jealous of their ability to get past their fertility issues. With us, it was the other way around. The more we tried to get pregnant, the more we got bogged down in our insecurities and became alienated. My frustration over not being the man you thought you were marrying turned into anger. You weren't the only one who threw up a wall between us."

"Leandros…" she said, sounding distressed. "If you don't mind, let's go inside. One thing I'm noticing about this pregnancy. I have to eat on time or I get famished."

He kissed the tip of her nose before getting out of the car to help her. He was famished, too, for *her*. But for the moment he had to be satisfied with this amount of detente, including the compliments she'd been paying him. Before she'd shown up in his office two days ago, he couldn't have imagined this much progress. Unfortunately, when they faced Karmela in the morning, there could be a setback that might undermine any progress they'd made.

At ten to nine the next morning, Kellie got out of the helicopter with Leandros's help and rode the elevator down to his office suite with him. She hadn't slept well during the night and had gotten up early to shower and wash her hair. After blow drying it so it fell in natural curls around her shoulders, she'd gone into the kitchen to take her pills and fix breakfast for the two of them.

After the fabulous seafood dinner with him the night before, she couldn't believe she was hungry again. Eating for three was no joke, but at this rate she'd have to start watching her weight. Already her clothes were fitting tighter. Pretty soon she'd need maternity outfits.

In order to feel comfortable, she'd put on a

cream-colored blouse with a khaki skirt that tied loosely around the waist. On her feet she wore bone-colored leather sandals. The doctor had warned her high heels weren't a good idea.

The way Leandros's eyes lingered on her while they ate on the terrace raised her temperature. His appeal was so potent, she was in danger of forgetting her own rule to keep her distance with him. But knowing they'd been through only one session of therapy, not to mention that they'd be confronting Karmela in a few hours, Kellie made certain she didn't succumb to him out of weakness. Instead, she got up and did the dishes before announcing she was ready to go.

No one was in Leandros's office when they entered on the dot of nine. She really hadn't thought Frato would be here, and was sure Leandros hadn't counted on it, either.

"Leandros? I'd rather wait outside the door with Christos while you speak to Karmela. I don't want her to feel like she's being attacked."

He caressed her cheek. "You're an amazingly kind person, Kellie. Tell you what. I'll record everything that goes on so you'll know exactly what was said. No more secrets, remember?"

She nodded and sat down next to his bodyguard to wait. Before Leandros disappeared into his office, she noticed how fabulous he looked in a tan suit and tie that accidentally matched her outfit. He was the picture of the successful CEO in charge of his domain.

There were times, like now, when she wondered how she'd been the one to catch his eye after Petra died. No woman was immune to him. Kellie's heart rate sped up as she imagined what was about to happen.

Leandros closed the door and went around his desk to buzz Mrs. Kostas. "Would you please send in Karmela?"

"Mr. Petralia! I thought you'd gone on vacation."

He smiled to himself. "I thought so, too. Where's Frato?"

"I haven't seen him yet. I'll send Karmela right in."

"Thank you." Leandros sat back in the swivel chair. "Good morning, Karmela," he said as she opened the door. "Come all the way in and sit down."

Karmela walked straight up to him. "Frato

told me about your conversation at the villa yesterday. I understand you want my resignation. But let me give you warning. So far he thinks he's the father of my baby. I'll go on letting him believe it as long as I can keep my job. If I can't, then we'll see how well you handle public opinion when news leaks to the press that you're the daddy."

What more proof did anyone need to know she was ill?

"If you're putting on this performance for me, it isn't necessary, Karmela. I have no idea if you're pregnant or not, but a pregnancy test demanded by a court order can clear that up in a matter of minutes. If you're pregnant, it couldn't possibly be my baby. A DNA test will provide the evidence, but surely you don't want to put Frato through that."

Leandros had seen that catlike smile on her face before. "Frato's more gullible than you. Why do you think the company made you CEO at your age? I'll tell him you and I were lovers during the times Petra was away on business. My family's yacht provided the perfect place away from everyone.

"Before you went to Rhodes on your new project, we got together. That was the time I conceived our baby. Three nights ago we were in this office alone for hours. All he has to do is check with Christos to believe me."

Leandros got to his feet. "I feel sorry for you and Frato. You need help to get over this obsession. It's tragic you've dragged my cousin into it. There's no more job for you here. If you'd like, I'll have your belongings sent to your parents' home."

When she made no move to leave, he paged Christos and asked him to come in.

"You wanted me?"

"Yes. Please follow Ms. Paulos to her desk so she can get her purse. Then escort her out of the building and put her in a taxi."

Her cat's eyes glimmered. She glared at Leandros. "You have no idea what you've done."

"On the contrary. It's the best decision for everyone concerned. Goodbye, Karmela."

As if nothing was wrong, she strode to the door and walked out, with Christos trailing her. The minute they left, Leandros rushed out into the hall to get Kellie and lead her inside.

She eyed him as he spoke to Mrs. Kostas over the phone. "I'm officially on vacation, but I'll be staying in Athens at the Cassandra. If you can't reach Frato, feel free to call me.

Karmela will no longer be working for us. See that her final paycheck goes to her parents' home on Andros Island. I'll be out of the office for the rest of the day."

"Yes, sir."

He shut off the speakerphone. "Before we leave, I'll play the recording so you'll know exactly what was said."

Kellie sat down to listen. When it ended, she looked up at him. "I don't believe for a moment she's pregnant with your baby, or even pregnant. She's like a defiant little girl. What a shame."

"I agree. All I can say is, thank heaven this is over." Leandros called for his car to be brought around the side of the building, his eyes blazing a hot silvery gray as they pierced Kellie's. "Let's get out of here. I want to take us for a drive around the residential neighborhoods in Athens. Maybe we'll see the house you'd hoped I would buy for your wedding present."

"Leandros..." Her voice shook. "After this scene with Karmela, how can you even think about anything else?"

"Very easily. Whatever she chooses to do or not do, we're through with her."

"I'd like to go back to the hotel."

His eyes scrutinized her. "I thought this confrontation meant we'd put Karmela to rest forever."

She shook her head. "I'm still reacting to what she said. Don't you understand? Even though it's not true, she has threatened to go to the media."

His mouth thinned to a white line. "*Even?* That means you're still not sure about me."

"Of course I am, but after her threat, I can't concentrate on anything else right now."

Leandros ushered Kellie inside the elevator and pushed the button. "If you can't, *I* can. With the twins coming, I want to get settled in the right place to raise them. If you've made up your mind to leave me no matter what, I still have to provide for them, and don't want them living in a hotel when it's my turn for visitation."

"I didn't say that!" She felt ill, especially after he'd done everything in his power to deal with Karmela and Frato since they'd left Mrs. Lasko's house. "Please give me some time, Leandros. Don't you realize how worried I am about the damage she could do to *you*?"

"That's not what's bothering you. A part of you is still worried about Karmela," he said in a wintry tone.

Silence reigned during their swift descent to the ground floor. He'd turned into his forbidding self, the side of him she'd seen toward the end of their marriage. It made it impossible for her to reach him. They walked to the car and he helped her in. When they drove out to the street, he said, "I'll drop you off at the hotel."

"No, Leandros. I've changed my mind and want to come with you."

"Why, since you won't be living with me? I'm going to use the rest of the day to look at houses with a Realtor. It could get too tiring for you. I may not find what I'm looking for today or tomorrow, but I can begin my search. If nothing suits, I'll buy a piece of property and hire an architect."

The Cassandra wasn't that far from his office. He pulled up in front and got out to help her inside the front doors, where people were coming and going. "I'll see you later." A nerve throbbed at the corner of his hard mouth. "Promise you'll call me if there's any kind of emergency."

"Leandros…"

"You may be carrying our children, but don't forget I helped put them there, and love them as much as you do."

Fighting tears, she grabbed his arm. "As if I could forget."

But he wasn't listening. "You already have a home picked out in Philadelphia. I need to find one for our children when they're with me."

I know.

His eyes were mere slits as he helped her to the elevator in the hall. He pinned her with an undecipherable glance before wheeling away. There was no extra squeeze or caress on the cheek. Why would there be when she was still behaving like the woman who'd insisted on leaving him?

Once he'd driven off, Kellie went up to their suite with a heart so heavy she wanted to die. Without hesitation she ran to her room and pulled the phone out of her purse to call Fran. It rang four times. *Please pick up.*

"Kellie? I've been hoping you'd call soon."

"Thank goodness you're there!"

"Hey…you sound frantic."

"I am. Nothing changes, does it?"

"Yes, it does. You're pregnant with twins! That makes three miracles for us."

Tears filled Kellie's eyes. "I know, but I'm still the same mess I've been for months. Can you talk?"

"Yes. My little miracle from out of the blue is in her swing, listening to the songs. I won't be feeding her for another half hour. Now's the time to tell me what's going on. You left me hanging yesterday. That wasn't fair."

"I'm sorry." Kellie kicked off her shoes and flung herself across the bed before she remembered she needed to be more careful. Slowly she turned over on her back and tucked a pillow under her head. Once she got started talking with her best friend, everything came tumbling out, until Fran was completely caught up.

"Deep down I always thought she was unstable, but I never dreamed Frato was involved."

"It's very sad."

"Hey, Kellie? What's going on? Please tell me you didn't believe Karmela's claim that she's carrying your husband's child!"

She shuddered. "No, but you never heard such a convincing performance in your life."

"Oh, Kellie... After everything that's happened, did you tell Leandros you still believe her?"

"I told him just the opposite!"

"But you left him in doubt by not going house hunting with him."

"I couldn't right then," she said defensively as tears scalded her cheeks.

"Then it sounds like she's won and you've lost the greatest man you'll ever meet on this earth. They don't come any finer than Leandros. I love you, Kellie, but I'm sorry for you."

Fran's comment was like a stab through the heart. "I'm going to hang up now."

"Don't do that! Talk to me! Surely learning about Frato's involvement with her explains everything. It should have made a new woman out of you! What's going on with you?"

"Honestly, it *has* removed every doubt I ever had, but I'm terrified of what she's going to do to him. The second Karmela left his office with Christos, Leandros acted like nothing traumatic had happened. After what she'd vowed to do, I couldn't imagine going anywhere."

"That's your husband, Kellie. He seizes the moment, then moves on. It's part of his brilliance."

"But Karmela is going to come after him!

It will cause terrible trouble in their families, just as Frato predicted. I know it."

"Obviously Leandros isn't worried about it. I'd say he's much more concerned about where the four of you are going to live."

"We're not officially back together. We still have other issues to work through. After the way I left him earlier, I don't know when he'll speak to me again."

"Just have faith that he will! You're the one who wanted counseling and agreed to do it here in Athens. Since he gave up his apartment, it's only natural he's anxious to find a place for the new family coming. Hotel living gets old in a hurry, even in one as posh as the Cassandra."

"I realize that, but I'm still reeling from what went on his office with Karmela. I don't know how he puts one foot in front of the other. Oh, Fran, I know I've hurt him again. He probably won't come back to the hotel until I'm asleep tonight."

"Maybe that's not a bad thing. It will give him time to cool off. Just remember he's a big boy and will get over it. You can discuss it with him in front of Mrs. Lasko at your session tomorrow. That's what marriage counseling is all about. What time do you have to be there?"

Kellie could hear little Demi making noises in the background. "At eleven. I think your daughter is getting hungry. I'll hang up so you can feed her."

"Okay. But before you go, you have no idea how thrilled I am that you're going to be in Athens for your therapy. I've missed you."

Kellie closed her eyes tightly. "Same here."

"Why don't we leave plans open for tomorrow? I'd love to have lunch with you, but depending on how things go at therapy, maybe the four of us could get together for a barbecue here at the apartment on the patio toward evening. Nik and I are dying to be with the two of you again. He told me to ask you to come over."

"I'll talk to Leandros and let you know. That is, if he's still speaking to me."

"Don't be ridiculous."

"Give Demi a kiss from me. Goodbye for now."

Kellie clicked off and rolled onto her stomach. The day's events had drained her. Unfortunately, the relief of knowing the truth about Karmela was overshadowed by the ugliness of her threats.

Kellie was afraid Leandros wasn't taking this seriously enough. Tomorrow she'd discuss this latest fear in front of their therapist. He would be forced to listen. If anything happened to him...

Tears crept out of the corners of her eyes before she knew nothing more.

CHAPTER SIX

AFTER SEEING KELLIE safely inside the hotel, Leandros drove over to his former apartment, feeling like a shellshocked victim. If his wife still harbored any doubts about him where Karmela was concerned, then their marriage truly was over. But until he calmed down, he wanted another talk with Frato.

Leandros didn't know what to expect, but he knew his cousin was in deep trouble and needed help. In order not to embarrass Frato further, this was one visit he needed to make without Kellie.

En route, he contacted a Realtor he knew well and asked him to come up with some houses to show him and Kellie later on. After he'd finished that call, Leandros phoned his attorney and brought him up to speed about the situation with Frato and Karmela. "I want you prepared for anything that might happen in the next few hours or days. Let's get some private detectives to put her under surveillance."

With that accomplished, he drove into the underground parking. He spotted Frato's BMW, but it didn't necessarily mean he was there. As for Karmela, she could be anywhere, drumming up trouble. She was impulsive, disturbed and furious. Leandros didn't know what to expect.

The second the elevator door opened to the penthouse, he saw Frato dressed in a robe, sprawled on the couch in the living room. He had one foot on the floor and had been drinking. His cousin had been doing more and more of that over the past few years.

"Frato? Where's Karmela?"

He squinted up at Leandros. "It's a cinch she's not here with me. I haven't seen her since all hell broke loose after I got back from Andros yesterday."

"For your information, more broke loose in the office this morning after I let her go. She threw out some expected and unexpected threats before I asked Christos to escort her off the premises."

At that news, Frato struggled to his feet with a groan. "You went in to work?"

"Someone needs to be running the Petralia

Corporation, don't you think? Don't worry. I covered for you and told Mrs. Kostas I was still on vacation. We're family, Frato, and we have to stick together. The last thing I'm going to do is fire you, but I need you sober. Go take a shower and get dressed for work while I fix you some coffee so we can talk."

While he waited, he phoned his electronics technician and asked him to come over and remove all codes except Frato's from the elevator security system. As Leandros clicked off, Frato reappeared. His cousin had done his best to disguise the fact that he was hungover.

"Who was that?"

"Not Karmela." After telling him he'd called the security technician to come, Leandros handed him a mug of coffee. "I'll explain why in a minute. Tell me the truth. Is Karmela pregnant with your baby? Is that why the rush to get married?"

The shocked look on Frato's face was all the explanation Leandros needed. With that question answered, he pulled out his cell phone. "I recorded everything the second Karmela walked through the door to my office." He turned it on and they both listened.

By the time they'd heard the door close behind Christos, Frato's tanned complexion had faded several degrees. With a trembling hand, he set down his empty mug.

Leandros switched off the recording. "I'm sorry you had to hear that, but it was necessary. She's got a serious problem, Frato. For a long time she's been using our weaknesses to play all of us against each other.

"You need to know I've already alerted my attorney. If you and I join forces, then whatever she tries to do to discredit us to the media or the families, we'll be a step ahead of her until she gets the help she needs."

He had never seen his cousin's brown eyes water like that before. "I can't believe what I just heard." Frato sank down on one of the bar stools. "What a damn fool I've been all these years."

Leandros patted him on the shoulder. "You don't want to hear what a damn fool I've been since I listened to Petra and gave Karmela carte blanche to do what she wanted. In my desire to placate Petra, I enabled Karmela in a way that has brought my marriage to Kellie to the brink of disaster. But we've started marriage counseling to try to save us."

"You're kidding...."

"No. Naturally it was Kellie's idea, because I've been too impossible to deal with."

"So that's what brought her back?"

Leandros shook his head. "She flew here to tell me in person that we're expecting twins next March."

Frato let out a long whistle that reverberated throughout the penthouse. "Twins? I'm beyond happy for you, Leandros."

His cousin sounded so genuine, it brought a lump to Leandros's throat. "I'm ecstatic myself. Kellie said I deserved to hear the news in person, but she still expected the divorce to go through. I told her I'd just made arrangements with you so I could fly to Pennsylvania, where we could go to counseling. After talking it over, we decided to do our counseling here. We've had one session already, with another one scheduled for tomorrow."

Frato's head jerked back. "Does Karmela know about this?"

"Not her or anyone. I want to keep it that way for the time being."

"Understood. Do you want the penthouse back?"

"It's yours, Frato, with my blessing. I found out Kellie never wanted to live here."

"Why not?"

"Because Petra lived here with me. Kellie wanted a place of our own, but I was too caught up in my desires to ask her what she wanted. Right now we're looking for a house."

"Incredible."

"Are you with me?"

"Yes!"

"Good. Together we can withstand any storm. When the families start calling you, pretend you know nothing. I suggest you get to the office so no one will suspect anything's wrong. Mrs. Kostas knows Karmela has been fired. She'll send her final check to her parents. While you dig into work, I'm going to enjoy my vacation."

Frato nodded. "I'm leaving now."

"One more thing. The technician is on his way over to delete Karmela's code from the elevator. When she calls because it's on the blink, tell her to find herself a good attorney, and assure her you'll have her things shipped to her parents."

As Leandros started to leave, Frato grabbed him and gave him a bear hug, the kind they used to share before their lives got complicated. "I swear I'm going to do better."

"I'll make you the same promise." He knew his cousin would hurt for a long time, but at least Frato's blinders had come off for good.

With everything taken care of for the time

being, Leandros felt an enormous weight had been lifted. He left for the hotel, eager to talk to Kellie and explain why he'd thought it was wise she remain there until he got back. His Realtor had called and left the message that he had some wonderful prospects for them, whenever they wanted to see them.

It was midafternoon when Leandros found her in her bedroom, sound asleep on top of the bed, resting on her side. She was still dressed in the skirt and top she'd worn to the office. Her shimmering gold hair was splayed across the pillow. There was no sign that she'd eaten lunch.

He stood in the doorway while his eyes devoured the sight lying before him. She was his whole world. Inside her delectable body their children were growing. They had a glorious future ahead of them. As badly as he wanted to lie down on that bed with her, he didn't dare. For once in his life he needed to practice patience and restraint in order to win back her trust.

"Leandros?" she murmured, after he'd turned to walk down the hall. "Is that you?"

He came back. "Who else?"

She sat up, trying to arrange her disheveled

hair. His wife reminded him of a tantalizing mermaid. "When did you get back?"

"Just now."

"It's four o'clock. I can't believe I slept this long."

"Jet lag has finally caught up with you. Did you eat in the restaurant?"

"No." She slid off the bed, causing her skirt to ride up her thighs before she stood. Kellie had no idea how desirable she was to him. "After I got off the phone with Fran, I fell asleep. Have you eaten?"

"Not yet."

"Then you must be starving, too. I'll order something from the kitchen for both of us."

"While you do that, I'll check my voice mail." He went into the sitting room, curious to see if there were any developments that needed immediate attention.

Dionne and Zera had both called. No surprise there. They wanted to know why Karmela had been fired. He moved on to the next call, from his Realtor.

"I've got a property in Mets. It's a taste of old Athens, with a tiled roof and a charming courtyard. Lots of flowering trees and shrubs of jasmine and bougainvillea. It's in one of the most beautiful neighborhoods and won't stay on the market long. If you're interested, I'll show it to you this evening, along with a couple of others."

Nothing could have pleased Leandros more. The last message came from his father, asking him to call him as soon as possible. As he clicked off, Kellie joined him. "Anything important?"

"I'll let you be the judge. From here on out, you and I are going to do everything together, so there won't be any more misunderstandings that could start another war." He replayed the messages for her.

Kellie looked shattered by his cousins' calls. "Karmela didn't waste any time, did she? It appears her family has already gotten to your father."

"I'll call him back after I've heard from my attorney. That might not be for another day or two. I want to be in possession of more facts before I touch base with him. He'll know how to calm down my mother."

"He's good at that."

A knock on the door alerted them that their dinner had arrived. Once the waiter had come and gone, they sat down to eat. "Shall I let the Realtor know we'd like to see those houses he phoned about?"

"Yes," she said unexpectedly. "This is a lovely hotel, but it's not a home. I'm sure you're anxious to get settled in something permanent."

Meaning she wasn't?

Her response left him feeling raw, but for once he wasn't going to erupt. Instead, he pulled out his phone and made arrangements with the Realtor that would keep them occupied for the evening.

Tomorrow would be their second therapy session. It couldn't come soon enough for him.

Olympia was already in her chair when Kellie walked into the room with Leandros at eleven. "Good morning, Mrs. Lasko."

"Good morning to you. Thank you for being on time."

Kellie gave the credit to Leandros, who had seemed equally anxious to get on with the therapy once breakfast was over. After they'd looked at four different houses the evening before—all of which she found had something wrong with them—he was up early on the phone with the Realtor, getting another list of houses for them to look at after their session.

"Please sit down."

Leandros helped her into the chair before he took his seat.

"Anything to report since our last session, before we get started?"

"Quite a lot, actually," Kellie blurted. She looked at Leandros. "Shall I tell her?"

"Go ahead."

Kellie explained about their meetings with Karmela and Frato. When she'd finished, Olympia eyed her in surprise. "I had no idea the results of our first session would produce anything as dramatic as what you've just described. Indeed, Karmela Paulos needs professional help.

"What's more important is that you've taken steps to remove the hornets' nest from your lives. It's an impressive start. I wish all my clients had results like yours within a forty-eight-hour period. Are you prepared to face what might come if she goes to the media in her rage?"

"My attorney is already working on it," Leandros stated with his usual confidence.

"In that case, why don't we begin with you. I'd like you to give me a picture of your life growing up on Andros. The mention of cousins came up in the last session. What part do they play in the family dynamic that has brought grief and makes them stand out?"

Since Olympia wrote no notes and didn't use a tape recorder, Kellie marveled at her photographic memory.

"We're a big family and all work in the Petralia Corporation. I have two living grandparents, but they've long since retired. My parents are semiretired. Though I'm an only child, I have five uncles and aunts, all married with children. I also have two great-uncles and aunts still alive with family.

"Of all the cousins, I'm closest to Frato. He's acting as CEO in my place while I'm on vacation right now. I have five boy cousins and six girl cousins, some older, some younger, two of whom have always been friendly with Karmela Paulos."

"So the joining of the Petralia and Paulos families at the time of your first wedding brought you all together even more intimately."

"Yes."

"All are well married, wealthy?"

"Yes."

"Including the Paulos family?"

"Yes."

"Except for Karmela, who's still single and delusional."

"Yes."

The older woman's gaze swerved to Kellie. "Now I want to hear about *your* upbringing." Olympia moved from subject to subject with a swiftness that made it hard to keep up.

Kellie cleared her throat. "My parents died when I was a baby, so I was raised by my mother's sister and her husband in Philadelphia. They weren't blessed with children, so it was the three of us. They're still alive."

"What does your uncle do for a living?"

"Before retirement, he was an insurance salesman who worked very hard. My aunt helped him. They were wonderful to me. As soon as I could, I got jobs while I went to school. My last year of high school, Fran and I went to school in France for an adventure. I paid for half of it, my uncle the other half.

"With student loans I made it through college, and continued to live with them in order to help them out. That's because my uncle suffered a stroke that put him in a wheelchair. It affected his legs, but not his mind. Once I graduated, I obtained a good position at an advertising agency. After working there for a year, the three of us decided to take our first trip to Europe.

"That was about two and a half years ago. When we flew here to Athens, we stayed at the Cassandra. One day while I was trying to get his wheelchair into the elevator, Leandros happened to be walking by, and helped me. That accidental meeting changed my life." Kellie couldn't prevent her voice from trembling.

"It changed both our lives," he declared with unmistakable fervency.

Olympia put her palms on the table. "I hope you've been listening to each other, really listening, because I want both of you to put yourselves in my role as a therapist. Imagine you're sitting in front of this husband and wife who've come to you. Their nationality, upbringing, social, economic and emotional standings are entirely different.

"The husband's parents are living. He comes from a big family with many tentacles, whose name is known throughout Greece. He's been married before to a socialite, but lost her and their unborn child in a tragic accident.

"The second wife has never been married, has never known her own parents and has committed herself to helping the aunt and uncle who raised her on a modest income without any other family around. She's in a country whose language and customs are unfamiliar to her.

"Kellie? Look at your husband and tell him the second emotion that came to mind when you told him you'd marry him. We already know the first one, that you were painfully in love with him."

Her mouth went dry, and her heart was thudding so hard she didn't know if she could get the words out. She turned and lifted her eyes to him. "I was terrified because I felt so completely inadequate in every way."

Leandros started to say something, but Olympia waved her thin index finger at him. "Your wife has just given you the key to understanding her. Do you remember the statement she made on Tuesday, about fearing she would never measure up to your first wife?"

"Yes."

"Now you can understand it was her feelings of inadequacy that made her feel intimidated. Before you override her comment with your well-meaning protests, sit back for a minute and let it sink in while I ask you a question."

His expression sobered.

"After she said yes to your proposal, what emotion drove you?"

In the quiet that followed, Kellie couldn't imagine what his answer would be.

"It's hard to put into words," his deep voice grated.

"Why?"

His gray eyes sought Kellie's. "Because I felt so many things."

"Name the dominant one."

She heard him take a fortifying breath. "Joy."

Kellie had felt joy, too. In fact, it had been overpowering.

"What manner did it take?"

His black brows furrowed. "I'm not sure I understand."

Olympia sat forward. "How did you manifest your joy?"

"I guess I wanted to give her the world."

Following his answer, Kellie started to tell him the world was the last thing she wanted, but Olympia stopped her with another warning finger. "It's your turn to sit back and think about what he just said, because it's the key to *his* personality."

Silence filled the room once more. Olympia eyed both of them. "There's no wrong or right here. What I see before me are two perfectly wonderful people who want the same thing. But you must follow what I'm saying.

"Leandros? Your problem is that you *can* give her the world, financially. You want to remove every obstacle from your wife's path and make her life easier. Being the confident male you are, with few insecurities, you sweep in and take over for the worthiest of reasons. But it makes you a poor listener and blind to certain facts sitting in front of you. In the end you come off seeming cold and insensitive."

He looked thunderstruck.

"Kellie? You have a different problem. You never knew your mother and father and had no siblings. Strictly speaking, Leandros was Petra's husband before he was yours. You couldn't get pregnant in what we consider the normal way. You're tired of not being able to claim anything of your very own. Not even the children growing inside you are strictly yours. All this has made you angry, with the result that your insecurity makes you distrustful and less than sympathetic."

A gasp escaped Kellie's throat. Olympia

had hit the nail so squarely on the head, she was astounded.

"It's no wonder that when insensitivity met up with distrust, you two reached an impasse in your marriage."

Kellie darted Leandros a glance and discovered him studying her intently through shuttered eyes. With Mrs. Lasko's help, it all seemed so clear what was wrong.

"Now let's analyze the positive. Though Kellie's insecurity caused her to ask for a divorce, Leandros, she threw you a lifeline by suggesting you go to marriage counseling. That's because she's a problem solver. She's had to be to make it through life this far. Consider that when she found out Karmela was working in your office, she asked if she could work there, too."

"In all honesty, my friend Fran gave me the idea," Kellie exclaimed.

Leandros darted her a shocked glance. "I didn't know that."

Olympia's brows rose. "The point is, you acted on it."

He got up from the chair with a bleak expression on his hard-boned features. "But I was too blind to understand what was happening, and turned you down."

"Your blindness was temporary," Olympia asserted. "You've been a winner all your life and aren't used to losing. Once separated from your wife without being able to do anything about it, you were humbled enough to realize that money and power couldn't help you obtain the one thing you wanted above all else. In your vulnerable state—a condition in which you've rarely found yourself—you grabbed the lifeline she tossed you, and agreed to go to counseling."

Kellie felt his penetrating gaze before he said, "It's a miracle you didn't tell me it was too late."

While a flood of emotions swept through her, Mrs. Lasko got to her feet, signaling the end of the session. "Before you leave, I have homework for you. Leandros? I want you to explore how you really feel about Kellie's best friend, Fran. I sensed resentment of her at our first session, but I want you to consider the fact that resentment masks jealousy."

"Jealousy?" he exclaimed.

"That's right. Why does she bring out that emotion in you?"

Kellie was so surprised by Olympia's comment, she didn't realize the therapist was now addressing her.

"As for you, Kellie, you not only feel guilt over your aunt and uncle's sacrifice, you feel as if you abandoned them when you married your husband, and are torn between two worlds. These issues need to be resolved in order to stabilize your marriage."

Hearing those words, Kellie bowed her head. How did Olympia understand so much?

"The more you dig, the more you'll begin to achieve that joy you first felt when you decided to make a life together. I'll see you on Tuesday. Goodbye."

On unsteady legs, Kellie got up from the chair and headed for the door. Leandros reached it first and opened it for her. He must have noticed she was shaken, because he cupped her elbow as he walked her out to the car, parked in the hot sun.

Before he put the key in the ignition he turned to her with a grim look on his striking Greek features. "Would you find me too insensitive if I told you I'd like to put off our plans for dinner with Fran and Nik this evening?"

Kellie drew in a deep breath. "I would have suggested it if you hadn't. What I'd really like to do is forget everything, including house hunting, and fly to Andros."

A light flashed in the recesses of those somber gray eyes. "You mean it?"

"Yes. We have so much to talk about, I hardly know where to begin. I'll call Fran right now and cancel."

"Do you think she'll be offended?"

"Disappointed, certainly, but not offended. It'll be fine." With Olympia's startling observations still spinning in her head, Kellie needed to show her husband that she put him first.

While he started the engine and they backed out to the street, she reached into her purse for her cell and pressed the speed dial. When Fran answered, Kellie turned on the speakerphone so Leandros could hear their conversation while they drove. *Everything out in the open.* Olympia's mantra.

"Kellie!" Fran sounded excited to hear from her. "How did the therapy go?"

She swallowed hard. "In all honesty, it was so heavy-duty this morning, I'm still reeling. Do you mind terribly if Leandros and I take a rain check for this evening?"

"You know better than to ask me that."

"Thanks for being so understanding." Kellie had almost said *thanks for being my best friend.* It was what she always said to her, oftentimes in Leandros's hearing. When she really thought about it, Kellie realized Fran had figured heavily in her life whether on or off stage. Not until this moment did it occur to her that Leandros needed to know *he* was her best friend.

The therapist had picked up on it, while Kellie had been oblivious. Was it possible that in some nebulous way, Leandros felt he came in second in her affections? Before the four of them spent any more time together, this was an area they needed to talk about.

"Fran? I'll call you on Monday."

"Take all the time you need. I'm not going anywhere. *Au revoir.*"

After she clicked off, Leandros turned to her. "If you're hungry for lunch, we can eat at the hotel before we leave for Andros."

She shook her head. "I'm still full from breakfast, but please don't let that keep you from ordering something."

"I'd rather wait until we reach the villa. I'll alert the housekeeper to get things ready for us."

In truth, Kellie had lost her appetite by the end of the session, and sensed Leandros wasn't any better off.

Without more talk, they returned to the

hotel to grab a few things and board the helicopter. The presence of his bodyguard further inhibited conversation.

During the flight her mind kept harking back to the conversation at their first therapy session with Olympia.

"Did you go to Rhodes without your wife?"

"Yes. Unbeknownst to me, she'd made arrangements for her best friend, Fran, to come to Greece."

"Best friend, as in Frato has been your best friend?"

"She's been like the sister I never had."

"They were going to take a two-week trip together while I was away on business. After making that announcement, she moved to the guest bedroom."

Kellie recalled the bleak tone in Leandros's voice, but she'd been too upset at the time to give it any real thought. It had taken this second session with the therapist for her to remember it, and it sent a stabbing pain of guilt through her.

Once they reached the villa and were finally alone, she followed him into the kitchen. He'd gone over to the sink and drank from the tap for a long time.

"Leandros?"

He slowly turned around, revealing a wounded expression. She took a step closer. "I'm so sorry."

Lines bracketed his hard mouth. "For what?"

"For making travel plans with Fran behind your back at the height of our marital troubles. It was cruel of me and made it impossible for you and me to communicate. But at the time I was too consumed with pain to realize what a selfish person I'd turned into."

She could hear her voice throbbing. The tears had started. She couldn't stop them. "I—I wouldn't blame you if you never forgave me for what I've done."

Heartsick, she hurried into the guest bedroom and lay down on her side, clutching one of the pillows to her while she sobbed.

"Kellie?" When she looked up, she saw him standing at the side of the bed. "There's nothing to forgive."

With tears dripping down her cheeks, she raised herself up on one elbow. "How can you say that? I used Fran to put a buffer between you and me."

"That was the only time I've ever been hurt by your friendship with her. Olympia caught it because she's good at what she does."

"You're not just saying that to make me feel better?"

"Why would I do that?"

"Because it's your nature to be kind." Kellie wiped her eyes with the back of her arm. "Olympia's a genius. She has me so figured out it's frightening."

His hands went to his hips. "Frightening?"

"Yes. She was right about my always having wanted something of my very own. When I met you, my heart and soul claimed you on some level I wasn't even aware of. After a life-long search, finding you answered the question of my existence. But knowing you had a history with Petra tortured me."

"Kellie..."

"It's true," she cried. "I grew too possessive of you. You were my best friend and lover. But instead of running to you with my fears, I held them in and became a shrew of a wife. Olympia's right. I *have* been angry, but the fault has lain with me. I'm so ashamed."

Convulsed in fresh tears, she buried her face in the pillow. Within seconds the mattress dipped and Leandros pulled her into his arms.

"I don't know how you can even stand to touch me," she moaned.

His answer was to pull her close. He felt so wonderful and substantial that she relaxed against him, having no desire to push him away as she'd done a few days ago. While in this halcyon state she heard familiar voices calling to Leandros.

Her eyelids flew open in surprise. "Your parents—"

Leandros kissed her temple before rolling away from her. "For them to walk in without phoning first, it means they're either tired of being ignored or they've heard the news about Karmela." As Kellie slid off the bed, he grabbed her hand. "Come on. Let's go talk to them."

"My skirt and blouse are wrinkled."

"I don't see anything wrong."

"Well, I should at least brush my hair."

"No. I love your mussed look."

Leandros. Her heart skittered all over the place.

They found his parents in the living room. Thea hurried toward Kellie and kissed her on both cheeks. "Forgive us for barging in, but we saw you arrive in the helicopter, and it's been too long," his mother cried. She was a beauty in her own right, a stylish and elegant brunette. "We've missed you, Kellie."

"Indeed we have." Leandros's father,

an aristocratic-looking man with salt-and-pepper hair, held out his arms to her.

"Vlassius..." She gave him a hug. "It's so good to see both of you."

He held on to her hands. "We retain Christos and Giorgios to keep our son safe. They were so happy to see you back in Athens, they let us know the moment you arrived at the office. You're a sight for sore eyes."

Kellie laughed. "I might have known they couldn't keep a secret, but at least they let me surprise Leandros in his own lair."

That brought more laughter.

CHAPTER SEVEN

"MY LAIR?" LEANDROS TEASED.

When he thought about it, he realized her remark was entirely apropos. After the desolate month he'd spent alone, her presence had been a surprise, all right. While he'd been hiding out in his office like a wounded animal licking his wounds, he'd suddenly heard her voice and seen his gorgeous blonde wife standing there like a vision. For a moment he'd thought he was hallucinating.

"Why don't you two join us out on the patio? We haven't eaten since breakfast," he said.

"Oh, no!" his mother exclaimed. "Let me help."

"We have it covered, *Mana*. Would you like to eat with us?"

"I don't think so. We only finished lunch a while ago."

In a minute he and Kellie took plates of

salad and rolls out to the wrought-iron table. The housekeeper had also prepared iced tea. They could all enjoy that.

After devouring a third roll, Leandros eyed his parents frankly. "Before you explode from curiosity, Kellie and I have a few things to tell you. Our divorce has been put on hold while we undergo marriage counseling."

Their eyes widened, but they didn't comment. He admired their restraint.

"It was Kellie's idea. I fought it at first, because you know me, I think I know everything."

His mother laughed. "I never thought I'd live to see the day when you admitted it."

"It takes a big man," his father interjected.

"Yes, it does," Thea joked, staring at her husband.

Leandros thought Kellie had to be enjoying this.

"As soon as I came back from the States alone, I realized I couldn't live without her, and finally agreed to it. But remember, we're not together." He eyed Kellie. "As our therapist says, we're a work in progress."

"Bravo," his mother exclaimed. But there was no bravo about it if Kellie believed Karmela's lie.

"I apologize for not having returned your phone call yet, but there've been reasons," Leandros went on. "As I informed you a few days ago, I'm on vacation. That's why I asked Frato to take over for me at the office. For your information, Kellie and I had our second session this morning."

Leandros darted his wife a glance. "We probably would have walked up to the villa to visit you later today." Kellie's nod confirmed it.

His mother clasped her hands together and let out a happy cry. His father smiled in obvious satisfaction. Their reactions had to have reassured his wife that they loved her. They'd been crushed when he'd told them Kellie was leaving him.

Leandros sent his wife another glance. If she wanted to tell them their other news, he was leaving it up to her. A hushed silence fell over the room. When it became deafening, he started to bring up another subject, but Kellie suddenly put her glass down and said, "Last week I went to my doctor in Philadelphia for a checkup and found out...we're expecting twins."

"Twins?" His mother was so ecstatic, she

jumped up from the table and ran around to hug him and Kellie again.

With tears in his eyes, his father followed suit. "This is a great day, a miraculous day!"

Thea's face was wreathed in a huge smile. "Two grandbabies to love. I can't believe it! Thank heaven for modern medicine."

"I can hardly believe the artificial insemination worked," Kellie admitted. "But the thought of taking care of *two* babies at once is pretty overwhelming."

"We'll all help," his mother assured her. "Your aunt and uncle must be thrilled. When are you due?"

"March seventh. They're nearly eight weeks old. The doctor said they're as big as blueberries, with tiny hands and feet emerging."

His parents laughed and cried. Inside, Leandros was thrilled, but until he knew unequivocally that Kellie believed in him, he couldn't celebrate the way he wanted. As for therapy, they still had a long way to go. The only thing helping him right now was that she'd let him hold her a little while ago. She'd even seemed to welcome his arms around her.

He waited until his parents sat down again before asking if there was another reason they'd walked down to his villa unannounced.

They shook their heads, clearly mystified by his question.

It meant Karmela still hadn't played her trump card. That's why he hadn't heard from his attorney. He was hoping that not hearing anything yet meant she might be backing down on her threats. If that was the case, then things couldn't be working out better.

"The therapy we've been undergoing has opened my eyes to a dangerous situation that was brewing long before we took our vows. Though we have other issues to work on, this has been one of the big ones threatening to undermine our marriage."

Both his parents frowned, but it was his father who demanded clarity. "Be explicit."

"As Kellie and I discussed earlier, there's been an enemy within our walls. Not only has she done everything in her power to come between Kellie and me, she's been doing an expert job of destroying Frato in the process."

"She?" his mother questioned, patently bewildered.

Leandros nodded grimly. "My former sister-in-law, Karmela."

The shock on his parents' faces convinced him they would never have suspected Petra's sister of any wrongdoing. They'd been completely in the dark about her.

"Kellie? Tell them what you told the therapist about the night of our wedding reception. My parents need to hear from you to understand what we've been up against. Don't leave anything out."

Once his wife began her tale, he watched their reactions. By the time she'd finished, he knew they were horrified.

"There's more," he said, pulling out his cell phone. "Once you hear this conversation between me and Karmela at my office, you'll realize what our family could be up against. Kellie has already listened to it." He switched on the recording.

While his parents sat there in shock, he eyed Kellie. He could tell she was worried about their reaction. When it had played out, he shut the device off.

"The girl's clearly unwell," his father declared.

His mother nodded. She looked ill. "What are you going to do, Leandros?"

"After I took Kellie back to the Cassandra, I went to the penthouse and had a serious talk with Frato. He's been in love with Karmela for a long time, but when he listened to this recording, it forced him to wake up. Frato's finished with her. If she tries to get into his penthouse, she won't be able to."

"Who would have dreamed she had such problems?"

"Maybe her parents *do* know, but haven't been able to help her. It's anyone's guess how far she's willing to take this. Dionne and Zera phoned to find out why I fired her, so she has revealed that much to those in the family who are sympathetic to her. But at this point, anything could be going on. Rest assured I've got her under surveillance and have alerted my attorney."

That didn't seem to mollify his father. "Has Frato told my brother all this?"

"I don't think so, Papa, but I could be wrong. They've always been close, but this business with Karmela is something Frato has kept hidden for years. I've advised him to go on doing his job at the office and say nothing."

"Well, there's something I can do!" His father pushed himself away from the table and stood up. "Let's go, Thea. We're about to pay a visit to Karmela's family right now. Let me have your phone, Leandros. They need to hear this so they can take their daughter in hand."

Leandros shook his head. "Though you

know the facts, I don't want you getting involved. You've been friends for too many years. I'm the one who fired Karmela, and she knows why. If anyone's going to talk to her parents, I'll be the person to do it. But it may not come to that. Should they contact you about this, then direct them to me. I want your promise on that."

His mother got up. "But if she should call one of the newspapers…"

Kellie darted Leandros a worried glance. "That's what I'm concerned about, Thea. Today's so-called journalists don't check their sources. Even if it's all lies, and your attorney forces them to print a retraction, the public goes on believing the lies. This could destroy your reputation and Frato's. The whole family could be hurt, including Karmela's."

"She's right," his father muttered. "With you two expecting twins, I don't like this at all. Does Karmela know about your miraculous news?"

"No. Besides you and her doctor, the only people aware are Kellie's aunt and uncle, our therapist, Frato, and Nik and Fran. For the time being, we'd prefer the rest of the family doesn't know about this."

"Understood. Come on, Thea. We're going to leave, to give you some privacy."

The four of them gravitated to the front door. After more hugs, his father said, "Even if you've got people watching Karmela, you need the security on you doubled."

"I've already taken care of it." Leandros eyed him solemnly. "I promise to keep you informed."

"See that you do. We're in this together. How long do you think you'll be staying on Andros?"

Leandros glanced at his wife. "We don't know yet."

His mother cupped Kellie's cheeks. "Whatever you do, wherever you go, you have to take extra special care of yourself now."

"I agree."

"I had two miscarriages before Leandros was born," Thea confessed. "After that, I was never able to get pregnant again." Her eyes misted. "Those babies you're carrying are extra precious."

"I know. Thank you for caring so much." Kellie kissed his mother again before his parents started walking away.

When Leandros couldn't see them anymore, he closed the door. Kellie had already gone out to the patio to clear the dishes. He had an idea she was trying to hide her emotions. Once he joined her, they got everything cleaned and put away in no time.

"Leandros?" She turned, resting her back against the kitchen counter. His body was on alert for any change of mood in her.

"What is it?"

"Would you like to go for a walk along the beach with me? I feel like stretching my legs."

This was the first time since she'd flown back from the States that she was the one asking him to do something with her. Excitement flooded through him.

He almost said, "I was about to suggest it, if you weren't too tired." But he'd learned his lesson. Because of therapy, he'd discovered she didn't like him hovering, let alone sweeping in and taking over. "I could use some exercise myself. Give me a minute to put on a pair of shorts."

Kellie didn't want to change out of her wrap-around skirt. It was the most comfortable piece of clothing in her wardrobe. First thing tomorrow she would go shopping. She needed some loose fitting tops and maternity jeans. Dr. Creer had warned her she'd grow bigger fast.

She went into the bathroom and brushed her hair before fastening it in a ponytail with one of her bands. Though it was late afternoon, the sun was still hot. After applying sunscreen and lipstick, Kellie went in search of Leandros. She found him in the kitchen on the phone, in his bare feet.

He'd changed into a short-sleeved, white cotton shirt left partially unbuttoned. In it and his navy shorts he looked better than any statue of a Greek god. Without her volition, a surge of desire for him welled up inside her.

Glancing up, he finally noticed her, and turned on the speakerphone so she could hear. The conversation with a man she didn't recognize ended soon enough. "That was the private investigator. Karmela's been staying at the Athenian Inn and hasn't left her room all day. He'll continue to keep me apprised."

"Leandros... Since we started therapy, you've let me listen in on every phone conversation. I know why you've been doing it, and I appreciate it. But it isn't natural or necessary. I trust you, and I believe that when you have something important to share with me, you will."

Some of the worry lines on his arresting face relaxed. "That works both ways." He put a couple of water bottles into a pack he fastened around his hips. "I don't want you to get dehydrated."

"Thank you for being so thoughtful." He was being so polite. *Too polite.* She knew why.

"You're welcome," he answered in his low, vibrant voice.

"Before we go, there's something I need to tell you."

"I know what it is."

"No, you don't," Kellie countered. "Petra was revered by everyone in your family. You wouldn't have fallen in love with her if she hadn't been a wonderful person. Unconsciously, I endowed Karmela with the same qualities.

"When she was in your office and declared she was pregnant with your baby, I honestly didn't believe her, but I was in shock to realize I was looking at a truly disturbed woman who isn't anything like her sister. That's why it took me getting out of there and going back to the hotel to see everything for what it is. I hope you can believe me when I tell you my doubts about her are gone. I do trust you. Completely."

"Thank heaven," he answered emotionally. "What do you say we take advantage of the sun?" Her husband never revisited a problem once it was over. He was such a remarkable man.

They left the villa. When they reached the sand, she removed her sandals and dangled them from her fingers while they walked in the opposite direction from the private pier. Kellie saw several boats in the distance. The light breeze was enough to fill their sails, so they skimmed along the shimmering blue water.

Paradise.

She had a lot on her mind and knew Leandros did, too, but neither of them spoke. Slowly they made their way around an outcropping of rocks. It led to a much smaller, sheltered cove where the hillside was filled with wildflowers. No villas had been built here so there were no people around. They had the thin stretch of beach to themselves.

"Leandros," she said tentatively, "I'd like to talk to you about something important."

"There are things I want to discuss with you, too."

"Then let's sit for a little while."

His brows furrowed. "You don't mind getting sandy in that skirt?"

"Not at all."

After she sank down, Leandros handed her a bottle of water. While she took sips, he put his own bottle to his lips and quenched his thirst. When he'd drained it, he stretched out on the sand and leaned back on his elbows. His dark wavy hair gleamed in the sun while he stared out at the water. Kellie got a suffocating feeling in her chest just looking at him.

"Leandros?" she whispered.

He turned on his side toward her. With his jaw set and his eyes shuttered against the sun's slanting rays, she couldn't read his expression, but sensed his emotions were raw. "What's on your mind?"

"Something Olympia hit on about my guilt over my aunt and uncle really touched a nerve with me. I was the luckiest girl in the world to be raised by them. When I married you, there was a part of me that felt like I was abandoning them. Because of that I suffered guilt, and didn't realize it could do so much damage."

His dark brows furrowed. "What do you mean?"

"If on our honeymoon I wasn't the same woman you'd fallen in love with, I'm afraid it was because I couldn't enjoy it completely, knowing they'd gone back to Philadelphia alone. The business with Frato's and Fran's observations about Karmela were only a small part of my inability to be myself with you.

"All this time I thought I'd hidden it from you, but when you told Olympia you knew something was wrong on our honeymoon, it really threw me. Hindsight is a wonderful thing, but in our case it has come too late."

Kellie felt his body stiffen. "Go on."

"I just want to explain why I didn't like any of the houses we looked at earlier. I know you liked the one with the tiled roof and the court-yard. I liked it, too, but—"

"But what?" He broke in tersely. "Just say what you have to say, Kellie."

"Do you remember when you were talking to me about the penthouse?"

His eyes, dark with emotion, played over her face. "How could I forget?"

"You said," she stammered, "you said that you would always have lived on Andros and commuted if Petra hadn't wanted to live in Athens."

"That's right," he muttered.

"Do you still feel that way? Please be honest."

"Kellie...I'm discovering we can't always have everything we want."

"In other words, you *would* prefer living on

Andros if everything else lined up the right way?"

In a sudden move, he got to his feet and stared down at her with a black expression. "What's this about? Are you trying to work up the courage to tell me you're going back to Philadelphia, so I can do what I want?"

"No!" she cried, and hurriedly stood up, shaking the sand from her skirt. "It's too soon to talk about anything like that. You're deliberately misunderstanding me."

"What else am I supposed to think?"

She put a hand on his arm. His body had gone rigid. "Why did you say we can't always have everything we want? Tell me."

He eased his arm away, as if her touch burned him. "Surely you know why. I'm aware of how crazy you are about Athens."

"I am. With all its history and monuments, it's a magnificent city. But I loved your home on Andros the first time you brought me here. When we were looking at houses with the Realtor, I kept thinking about your villa. No place else in the world could possibly compare. It's no wonder you love it so much. To buy or build a home in Athens is ludicrous when this is the only home where the children should live and be raised."

"You honestly mean that?" She heard a tremor in his voice.

"Yes. Their heritage is here with their grandparents and relatives."

Kellie heard him struggle for breath. "Their heritage is in Pennsylvania, too. Don't think I don't know how torn you've been over being separated from your aunt and uncle. I always wanted them to move to Greece, but you said no. I didn't need to hear Olympia's thoughts on the subject to realize how hard it's been for you."

"That's because I know my aunt. She's afraid my uncle wouldn't want to leave their friends. There's also the issue of his health care companion, and whether my uncle could adapt to a new environment. Unfortunately, my thinking has been foggy because of all my hang-ups. But therapy has made me see I've been a fool. I've missed them terribly and realize they've missed me, too. Naturally, I've been their whole world since my parents died. Nothing else has been as important to them."

"I'm glad you finally understand that."

She nodded. "Leandros...if we make the decision to stay together, I want to live here year-round."

He looked thunderstruck. "You love it that much?"

"I might not have been born here, but I love it probably as much as you do. Olympia was right about me. I do crave something of my very own. Since you told me Petra had never lived in the villa with you, that changed everything for me. I know now there was no third party on our honeymoon. I feel like we could start a new life here, built on a firm foundation. But—"

"But you couldn't do it without your aunt and uncle living here, too," he finished for her.

"Yes."

"I've always been aware of that. We need them with us. So will our children. Otherwise we'll never be completely happy. Come on. On our way back to the villa, we'll take a detour. I want to show you something."

After putting their water bottles in his pack, he grasped her hand and held it tightly. Kellie could feel her husband's excitement. He came alive as they retraced their steps around the point to the next cove. When they reached the path leading away from the beach, she slipped her sandals back on. They followed it until it diverged. He took the trail to the right until they came to a small stone villa.

"Wasn't this your great-uncle Manny's house?"

"That's right. His wife died while I was in college. They never had children. Since his death a year ago, it has stood empty." Leandros reached for a key left above the lintel, and let them in the side door. It led into the kitchen.

"I remember being in here before. It's very cozy and charming."

"With some renovations, I believe your aunt and uncle would be very happy here. It's all on one floor and would accommodate his wheelchair. We'd hire a housekeeper to take care of them so they could maintain their independence."

"Oh, if I thought this were possible..."

"Of course it is. If there's a drawback, it's that they'd be surrounded by my relatives. But we'd provide them with a car, so they could drive to the different villages, or go visiting whenever they wanted company."

Kellie's eyelids prickled with salty tears. "This would be a perfect place, but I'm sure your family would have something to say about it."

Leandros grasped her upper arms, bringing her close to his hard-muscled body. "Dozens of people with a lot of money have coveted this villa, sitting on the most prime property of the island. My father and uncles have had dozens of offers to buy it, for many times what it's worth. But they haven't wanted anyone who wasn't family to live here on the estate."

"I can understand that."

"They'd rejoice if your aunt and uncle made this their home. You're family, after all. My extended family will celebrate, anyway, when they hear we're expecting twins."

"You're g-generous beyond belief, Leandros." Her voice caught. "I've never known anyone like you."

She felt his gaze narrow on her mouth, but he held back from kissing her. For once she wished he would devour her the way he used to do, but she'd changed all the rules when she'd asked for a divorce. He was much more careful now. Kellie sensed he was waiting for her to initiate any intimacy between them, because he didn't want to make more mistakes.

Neither did she.

Afraid she'd killed something inside him, she turned away with an ache in her heart, and started for the door. On the way back to the villa, he suggested they drive to one of the other villages to eat dinner. He said it so airily, the tension-filled moment in the kitchen, when she'd wanted to pull his head down to hers and give in to her desire, might never have happened.

On impulse, she said, "I have another idea. Why don't you start up the grill on the patio and I'll make us some lamb kabobs." He loved them. "I'll be able to marinate them for only a few minutes, but they'll still taste good. We'll finish off the salad and rolls, too."

"You really want to cook tonight?" He sounded eager, yet once again she noticed he was careful not to ask her if she was too tired. What had she done to him?

"Absolutely."

I want to do something for you.

Kellie hadn't made a meal for him in over two months. A Greek man loved his food. Leandros had always liked finding her in the kitchen while she cooked up a storm. When he'd claimed in front of Olympia that he'd loved coming home to Kellie after work, she knew he hadn't been lying about that. Because of therapy, she realized he'd never lied to her about anything.

"Make a lot of them," he called out before disappearing into the house.

She smiled, remembering the dozens of times he'd said the same thing to her when he'd phoned her from work, telling her he was coming home.

After washing her hands, she got busy. As she assembled the ingredients, it occurred to her she hadn't ever been this happy before. This was her kitchen. She was making dinner for her husband. They were pregnant with twin babies. He'd just told her they would move her aunt and uncle to the estate. Except for news about Karmela's next move still hanging over them, Kellie had more joy than any one woman deserved or could hope for in this life.

She was in the middle of her preparations when Leandros came back into the kitchen with his phone in hand. Judging by the lines bracketing his eyes and mouth, the news was bad.

"Who just called you?"

"The private detective."

"Did Karmela elude him and get to the press, anyway?"

Leandros inhaled sharply. "No. She managed to fix it so they got to *her.*"

"What do you mean?"

"She's even more devious than I realized. After overdosing on some pills at the hotel, for the sake of theatrics, she called the police so they'd be certain to find her before she could do any real damage. The private detective was out in the hall when the paramedics arrived. He followed them to the hospital, where her stomach was pumped.

"He spoke to one of the officers who heard her statement. She said I ended our affair after finding out she was pregnant with our baby, and fired her from the Petralia Corporation. The news will leak out. It always does."

Somehow Kellie wasn't surprised. "Even if it makes the ten o'clock news, it won't matter," she declared. "Anyone who knows you will realize she's a very sick girl who needs a psychiatrist. Let's get to the hospital. Call your parents so they can fly to Athens with us. It'll be better if we're all together when we talk to her parents. I'll phone Frato. He'll want to meet us there."

Leandros's eyes pierced hers. "You're willing to come with me?" he asked in a grating voice.

She knew what he was asking. Besides everything else, they might have to face a barrage of reporters. If ever they needed to present a united front, it was now. "Yes. I'm your wife. We do everything together."

"Kellie..." For once he forgot the rules and

crushed her in his arms. She clung to him before he was forced to let her go and alert Stefon to get the helicopter ready. While Leandros changed clothes and made the call to his parents, she phoned Frato. To her relief, he picked up fast.

"Kellie?"

"Yes. Please listen. Where are you?"

"I'm at the penthouse."

"Then you don't know about Karmela yet."

"What's happened?"

Once she'd explained, he said, "I'll phone Father, then head on over to the hospital and meet you there."

"Good. If we're all together, it'll be the best statement we could make."

"Agreed."

After they hung up, she made a couple of sandwiches for them to eat on the helicopter and put the uncooked food in the fridge. Leandros appeared in the kitchen wearing a gray suit and tie. "Ready?"

"Almost." She wrapped the sandwiches. "Here, take these." While he found a sack and added some apples, she went to the bathroom to freshen up. Moments later they hurried out of the villa. She didn't worry about the coals in the grill. They would burn down.

Her thoughts were on a real fire burning out of control at the hospital in Athens. Kellie loved her husband desperately, but never more than at this moment, when his life and reputation were at the mercy of Karmela.

CHAPTER EIGHT

LEANDROS TOLD STEFON to land at the hotel. From there, he drove the four of them to the hospital. There was a delivery entrance on the south side of the building. Hoping to avoid the paparazzi, he called for permission to park there, and a security guard allowed them to enter the building.

Frato had just phoned and told Leandros to go to the psychiatric unit on the third floor, west wing. He'd be waiting for them in the lounge off the hallway. To his knowledge, the police had notified Karmela's parents, who were still inside the locked area with the doctor.

Kellie held on to Leandros's arm, the way she'd done in the early days of their marriage. He hardly recognized her as the same woman he'd brought to this hospital five weeks ago, after she'd fainted. That woman wouldn't let him touch her.

He wanted to believe she was aching for the intimacy they'd once shared, and that's why she was clinging to him. If this show of solidarity in front of everyone didn't extend beyond this hour of crisis, he didn't think he could bear it.

"Leandros..."

Frato's parents had just appeared, but he'd been too deep in his torturous thoughts to realize it. Kellie got up first to greet them. Soon Leandros's parents had gathered around. While they were huddled together discussing Karmela's sorry state, the door opened and her parents emerged, white-faced. Leandros thought they'd aged ten years.

Kellie was right with him as they walked over to embrace them. "How is she, Leda?"

"Sedated. We can't see her again until tomorrow morning." Karmela's mother lifted tear-filled eyes to him. "She's always been crazy about you, Leandros, but we hoped and prayed she'd get over it after you married Kellie. If anything, it made her worse, but we had no idea she would try to kill herself."

Leandros's heart went out to them. "Just remember one thing. She called the police so they'd be sure to find her in time."

Nestor nodded. "The doctor said it was a

call for help. She didn't want to die. She did it to get your attention. We're so sorry for the grief she has caused you and Kellie... and Frato." He eyed Leandros's cousin with compassion before looking at Leandros again. "Are you two back together?"

He sucked in his breath. "We're working on it. I can tell you with conviction that with enough love and therapy, she'll get through this."

"You really believe that?" Leda's voice trembled.

"We do," Kellie interjected. "We're going to counseling right now. It's been a liberating experience for both of us. I'm sure it will be for Karmela, too."

Leda hugged Kellie. "You deserve all the happiness in the world."

"So does Karmela."

"You can say that after everything's she's done? What we heard her tell the doctor horrified us. But a pregnancy test was done. She's not pregnant."

"We didn't think she was. From what I've learned, she's been in pain for years, Leda. The doctor will help her understand that pain, and then she'll get well."

"Bless you." Leda hugged Kellie again.

Nestor eyed all of them. "The second the police called, I asked them to do all they could to prevent this from leaking to the press."

Leandros patted him on the shoulder. "Don't worry. If there's fallout, we can handle it. One thing you could do is put the record straight to Dionne and Zera. They love Karmela. She'll need their friendship more than ever now."

Leda nodded. "We'll call them before we go to bed."

In an automatic move, Leandros put his arm around his wife's shoulders. "Since there's nothing more we can do here, we'll go. Keep in close touch with us. You know we'll do whatever we can to help."

After more hugs, they said good-night to Frato and his parents, then the four of them left and drove back to the hotel. It was decided his parents would stay the night. Tomorrow they'd fly back to Andros.

Once ensconced in the suite, Kellie made coffee and ordered more food from the kitchen. They all needed time to settle down and relax before they could think about bed. It was better this way.

Leandros was on fire for his wife, but until she showed him she wanted him, body and soul, he wasn't about to push anything. In fact, this would be a good time to broach the subject foremost on his mind, now that Karmela was finally getting the help she needed.

He sat back in the chair, eyeing his parents over the rim of his coffee cup. "Kellie and I have been doing a lot of talking. Since our wedding, she's suffered over missing her aunt and uncle. We've flown to Philadelphia when we could, but traveling there every few months hasn't been enough. It's been harder for them to come here, because he's in a wheelchair.

"Yesterday, while we were out walking, I made a decision." Kellie's head jerked toward him in surprise. "If we agree to stay together, it will depend on her aunt and uncle where we live permanently."

The room went perfectly still.

"Kellie has been worried, with good reason, about uprooting them to live in Greece. They've built a lifetime of memories and friends in Philadelphia, and the move might be too hard on them. This last month she put down earnest money on a house big enough for them and our children. We would all live there."

His mother shook her head in consternation. "But what would you do?"

"I could still work for the corporation long distance. Naturally, I'd step down as CEO."

"And then you'd come and visit us every few months...." His mother's mournful voice trailed off.

"Nothing's written in stone yet, *Mana*. If Kellie and I decide to stay together, and if by some miracle they'd be willing to move here, then we'd live on Andros permanently."

"Permanently?" A squeal of joy escaped his mother's lips before she got up from the couch. "Then we'll make that miracle happen! Your aunt and uncle will be so welcome here, they won't have time to miss people. Think how busy we'll all be when the children are born!"

She flew across the expanse to hug him. "I hated it when you moved to that penthouse in Athens."

"I did it for Petra."

"We know you did, but nothing's been the same since." She moved to Kellie, seated in the other chair. "You really want to live on Andros?"

"It's my favorite place in the world. The

children will thrive there." Kellie's heartfelt response made its way inside his heart and convinced his parents. His mother squeezed her.

"Did you hear that, Vlassius?"

His father's eyes had glazed over with happy tears. "I heard. I'm still trying to take it all in."

"So what can we do to get your aunt and uncle to come, Kellie?"

Leandros sat forward. "On our way up from the beach yesterday, we stopped to look at Uncle Manny's villa. How do you think the family would fee—"

"It would be perfect for them!" his mother cried out, before he could finish his thought.

His father nodded. "I go fishing every morning on the boat. Jim will come with me."

"And Sybil will come shopping with me!" his mother exclaimed.

"Family should be together and that place shouldn't go empty any longer," his father declared. "With twins on the way, I think it's the best idea you've ever had."

"You're the most generous people on earth," Kellie declared in a tremulous voice. "I guess you realize your son takes after you."

Leandros liked the sound of that. "Though it seems like a perfect arrangement to us, everyone in the family would have to be in agreement. The villa needs work. I'd want to make improvements to the bathroom."

"I can tell you right now the family will welcome the idea without reservation."

"Thanks, Papa. However, if there is a problem, then there's still room on my piece of the property to build a new villa for them. But until Kellie talks to them about moving to Greece, it's a moot point, considering we're still in the middle of therapy."

His father stood up. "Come on, Thea. Let's go to bed and plot."

Kellie laughed out loud. It was the full-bodied kind he'd missed hearing all these months.

He eyed his parents. "That's a good idea. I'm suddenly exhausted and crave sleep. Everything you need should be in the guest bedroom. We'll see you at breakfast."

Taking a leaf out of their book, he got up and walked over to Kellie. "Get a good night's sleep." He kissed her on the cheek. "See you in the morning."

His heart leaped to see the look of disappointment in those chocolate eyes before he headed for his room. But he was doing better at disciplining himself where his wife was concerned. He wanted her to come to him, day or night, of her own free will. No holding back.

The apartment had gone quiet. Feeling wide-awake, Kellie carried the coffee mugs to the kitchen. She was still in shock that Leandros had gone to bed so fast. After what had happened today, there was so much she wanted to talk to him about, but by leaving the living room with his parents, he'd made any more conversation tonight impossible.

She knew she could always go to his room, but he would take that to mean she wanted to be with him in every sense of the word. Of course, she wanted that more than anything in the world. But when the moment came that they decided to recommit to each other, she preferred to be strictly alone with him on Andros.

Since arriving in Greece, Kellie had done so much sharing with her husband, she hardly recognized the person she'd become. Without him being available, her normal impulse would have been to phone Fran and talk to her about everything, disregarding the lateness of the hour. But that was before the therapy sessions. The revelations they'd uncovered had changed Kellie's life. She was turning into a different person.

When she really thought about it, her only real concern at this point was her aunt and uncle. If they could have seen and heard the reaction of Leandros's parents tonight, it would have warmed their hearts to know how much they wanted them to move to Greece.

Kellie checked her watch. It would be afternoon in Philadelphia. Now would be the best time to call them and have a long talk. After getting ready for bed, she climbed under the covers and picked up the receiver on the bedside table.

"Aunt Sybil?"

"Honey..."

"Have I caught you at an inconvenient time?"

"Heavens, no! I'm just putting the raspberry jam I made into the freezer. You know how much Jim loves it. We were just talking about you at lunch, wondering how the therapy is coming along. Are you still suffering nausea?"

"No. The medicine Dr. Creer prescribed

has really helped. Listen, there's something very important I need to talk to you about."

There was a small silence before she said, "You sound excited."

"It's more than that, Aunt Sybil. Could you get Uncle Jim to pick up the extension in your bedroom?" They were one couple she knew who didn't use cell phones.

"Just a minute. He's out on the terrace. I'll wheel him into the bedroom. Hold on."

Kellie's heart was pounding so hard, she feared it couldn't be good for her, but there wasn't anything she could do to slow it down.

"Is that you, Tink?" Her loving uncle had called her his golden Tinker Bell from her childhood. "How's the therapy going? Are you making any progress with this Mrs. Lasko?"

Tears filled Kellie's eyes. She loved them so much. "To make a long story short, Leandros and I are finding our way back to each other."

Sounds of pure joy reached her ears.

"I'm going to tell you everything that's happened. Then I need to ask you a question, and you have to answer it honestly, because I love you more than anything in the world and want you to be as happy as you've made me all these years."

The silence that followed let her know

she'd captured their attention. Getting in a more comfortable position, she began her tale. Leaving out their biggest problem, which had to do with artificial insemination and their struggle to get pregnant, she got into the ins and outs regarding Karmela and Frato.

Next she told them about Leandros's relationship with his first wife, and the many misconceptions Kellie had drawn throughout their marriage. Finally she explained why Karmela was now in the hospital, hopefully getting the kind of help she needed.

"That brings me to the one of the issues in our marriage we still haven't resolved."

"You mean there's more?" her aunt asked in a quiet voice.

"Yes, and it has to do with the two of you."

"What do you mean?"

"Leandros loves you and wants all of us to be together on a permanent basis. If you feel you could never leave home, then he's ready to step down as CEO of the company and move to Philadelphia."

She heard her aunt's gasp.

"I've told him about the house in Parkwood. I already have earnest money down on it. Since you've seen it, you know the place is big enough to accommodate the six of us after the children are born. We'll turn one of the upstairs rooms into a study for Leandros. He'll do business for the corporation from there."

"But—"

"Don't say anything yet, Uncle Jim. Let me finish. Here goes. We've decided that if you're willing to move to Greece, we'll make our permanent home at his villa on Andros Island and commute to Athens by helicopter."

"Honey—"

"I'm not through yet, Aunt Sybil. There's a small, vacant villa only a two-minute walk from his. It belonged to his uncle Manny until he died last year. Thea and Vlassius live only a three-minute walk from the villa in the other direction. We'd all be together! With the babies coming, it would be heaven."

She heard sniffing, but didn't know if it was a good or bad sign.

"Leandros has already talked to his parents about the renovations we'll have done to make you two as comfortable as possible. It's a darling, cozy house with the most glorious garden and fruit trees. The beach is only steps away."

"Tink—"

"We'll hire a person to help you," she talked

over him. "It won't be Frank unless he's willing to relocate with you. If not, we'll find someone equally wonderful. There's a small swimming pool on the side of the villa where you can do therapy. The temperature of the air and the water is perfect. Vlassius will be thrilled to take you fishing every morning on his boat, Uncle Jim. Now he'll have someone to go with him."

Her uncle made a croaking sound.

"You'll have your own car, Aunt Sybil. You and Thea can go shopping all the time. We'll take you to visit all the sites and museums. You can browse to your heart's content in all the little villages. And something else about Thea. She's a homebody like you who loves to cook and have family around. There are a bunch of Petralia family members living on the estate. You'll love all of them.

"In fact, I think you'd be shocked how much you have in common with them. We'll get you started learning Greek. By the time the babies are born, you'll be able to converse and understand almost everything. We'll become a bilingual household."

"Kellie," her aunt interrupted her. "You've convinced us it all sounds like a dream come true, but you don't need to go to these lengths because we're perfectly content here."

That was her aunt's stubborn side talking. "If that's your final answer, then I won't say any more about it. But since I'll never be truly content away from you, then Leandros and I will be moving to Philadelphia."

"Then *his* parents will be alone—" her uncle blurted.

"In terms of his being their only child, that's true. But they have brothers and sisters living on the island. They're not in your situation where you've never had family to call on. Of course, they'll fly to the States to visit us whenever possible. Leandros is determined to make this work, because he loves you."

Kellie heard her uncle clear his throat. "We love him…. Sybil? We can't expect Leandros to move here. He's an important man with a job to do." His words caused Kellie's heart to run away with her again.

"I know. I'm only thinking of you, Jim." Her aunt's voice trembled.

"Fiddle faddle. Moving to Greece will be a new adventure for us. Before my stroke, we'd planned to spend a lot of time traveling."

"You can still travel, Uncle Jim. The helicopter will take us everywhere. You can invite your friends to visit."

"Well, that settles it for me. If you want to know the truth, Sybil, I don't want to miss a day of watching our grandbabies grow up. Do you?"

Her aunt had broken down crying. "No."

By now Kellie was dissolved in tears herself. "You two don't have any idea how happy you've made me. Throughout our marriage, Leandros has worried continually about you, but no longer. I can't wait to tell him."

"Do you have any idea how different you sound?"

"All I know is how I feel, Aunt Sybil. I'm so deeply happy on every level, I'm afraid I'm going to burst."

"We don't want you to do that. It's awfully late for you to still be up, honey. You need to take care of yourself and get to bed."

"I will. The next time I call, I'll put Leandros on the phone and we'll start making moving arrangements. In the meantime, decide what you want to bring to your new house. Love you. Good night."

After hanging up, Kellie turned on her side. Oblivion took over while she was imagining when and how she would tell Leandros. It had to be the perfect time and place.

Leandros had just finished shaving when he had a call from his attorney. "Turn on your TV to the nine o'clock *Athenian Morning Show*. I've heard they're doing the story on you this morning despite my attempt to quash anything about you. Call me when it's over and we'll plan a damage strategy."

There was no such animal. Karmela had always been one step ahead and hadn't missed a trick. On a burst of adrenaline, Leandros reached for the TV remote and got in on the last of the weather forecast. Hot and sunny.

"Welcome, everyone. Thanks for tuning in to the *Athenian Morning Show*. Once again the Petralia Corporation is in the news. Five weeks ago a tornado swept through Greece, taking lives and destroying part of the Persephone, their newest resort outside Thessalonika.

"Today we bring you our top story involving the attractive thirty-five-year-old CEO himself, Leandros Petralia, who's been involved in a scandal that has rocked the country. He's been unavailable for comment since the news broke that his striking sister-in-law,

Karmela Paulos of the Paulos Manufacturing Company, and one of the secretaries at the Petralia Corporation, is carrying his child.

"Frato Petralia, a cousin who's vice president of operations, has been installed as acting CEO of the corporation while they attempt to weather this crisis. A reliable source has informed the station that his second marriage, of two years duration to Kellie Petralia, his American-born wife, fell apart because of the affair.

"She's divorcing him for an undisclosed amount of money. If you remember, his first wife, prominent beauty Petra Paulos, who'd been working for Halkias Textiles, died four years ago in a tragic plane accident along with their unborn baby. More on this story and pending lawsuits will be reported in tonight's news.

"Moving on to another scandal involving one of Greece's major banks..."

Furious for what this could do to Kellie, Leandros shut off the TV and got dressed. He was on his way out of the room when his phone rang again. Seeing the caller ID, he picked up eagerly. "Nik?"

"I'm glad you answered. It's good to hear your voice. I'm just sorry to learn about your precarious circumstances. My brothers both phoned to tell me about the horrendous lies put out on the morning news. How can Fran and I help? She's beside herself for the two of you. Frankly, so am I. You don't need this while you're both still in counseling. Karmela's form of sabotage leaves a taint no matter how you try to squelch it."

"It's ugly, all right, but Kellie and I are far enough along in our therapy to have surmounted most of our difficulties, and we know the truth."

"Thank heaven for that."

"Tell Fran not to worry. My wife will be calling her shortly to explain. I'm afraid we're just going to have to ride this storm out. Talk to you later. Thanks for your support, Nik. It means everything."

Leandros hurried out of the bedroom and down the hall. Kellie's door was still closed. It could mean she was still asleep, or maybe she was already on the phone to Fran. Practicing patience wasn't his forte, but once more he held back from joining her, and headed for the living area. He found his parents enjoying breakfast at the dining room table.

His father looked up. "Did you catch the news on TV this morning?"

"Afraid so."

"It's pure tripe."

Nerves twisted his insides. "Have you seen Kellie yet?"

"I'm right behind you."

He wheeled around to discover his wife dressed in the same blouse and skirt she'd worn here last evening. His heart raced at the sight of her beautiful face and body.

She eyed him intently. "I watched the news, too. You have to hand it to Karmela. With her smarts and energy channeled in the right direction, she could do wonders with anything she set her hand to."

His spirits plunged. "I wish you hadn't seen it."

Her smile disarmed him. "Leandros... We knew she'd do her worst. She wove just enough truth into the lies to make it sound authentic. You and your attorney probably have a plan to deny the allegations. But if you want my opinion, I think we should just leave it alone and go on living our lives."

"Oh, I agree!" his mother declared.

His father followed with a "Bravo!"

Leandros drew in a fortifying breath, relieved by his wife's response. "Then the four of us are on the same page."

Those brown eyes shone with a new light. "I've given up on the news stations doing their research and getting documented proof about anything anymore. People who want to believe the worst always will. If you lose business, you wouldn't want them for clients under any circumstances. In time even *they* will realize the story had no substance to it. Unless you have other plans, I'd like to fly back to Andros."

"Not without breakfast, you don't," his mother exclaimed. "Sit down. There's plenty here for both of you."

Suddenly his appetite had come back. He helped Kellie into the chair, tantalized by her alluring fragrance. "You look rested. I take it you got a good sleep."

"The best I've had in months. How about you?"

As he took his place next to her, a prickling sensation broke out on the back of his neck. Something was different about her. He glanced at his parents. "Do you want to fly back with us?"

"No. We're going to stay here until tomorrow," his father stated. "We'll be meeting up with some of the family later. You two go on."

Anxious to get away from the paparazzi

who'd spring at them at every opportunity, he phoned Stefon to get the helicopter ready. Thankfully, he'd doubled the security on Andros to keep them off his property.

Within ten minutes they'd kissed his parents goodbye and were on their way. En route he phoned his attorney and told him there was nothing to be done for now. After thanking him, he made a call to Frato, who'd insulated himself with extra security so he could get his work done.

His cousin seemed to be in surprisingly good spirits considering his pain over Karmela's betrayal. Frato wasn't taking any calls except from his family and Leandros. He did want to know when Leandros planned to return to work.

There was no way to answer that question. If he and Kellie got back together—and that was still an if—then there was a distinct possibility they'd be living in the States. But he was afraid to speculate that far ahead. Though he knew they were making progress in terms of understanding their conflicts and doing something about them, he didn't know if she could bring herself to live with him again. That's what this was all about.

The history they'd been through might have

been too painful for her to allow herself to be open and vulnerable to married life once more. That he'd been too blind in certain areas and too inflexible on occasion had done a lot of damage. To live with him on faith, hoping he'd catch himself when he was in danger of falling into old habits, was a lot to ask of her. Maybe too much.

Until further notice he'd remain on vacation. Next week was their third counseling session with Mrs. Lasko. A month ago he'd fought the idea of allowing anyone to get into his private thoughts, let alone be willing to listen to any constructive criticism. He found it amazing that in just a few visits, he welcomed any insights their therapist offered that would help in bringing him and Kellie back together.

When the helicopter touched down and they'd made their way to the villa, Kellie turned to him. "Do you think it would be all right if we drove into Chora? I realize there'll be reporters lurking, but I'd like to buy some maternity clothes. This skirt is the only thing that feels comfortable. My jeans are too tight."

Her request sent a burst of excitement through him. For once he'd been caught off guard and ran a possessive eye over her curvaceous figure, when he'd promised himself he wouldn't. As a result he almost didn't answer her question. "I've hired enough extra security to make certain we're not bothered."

"You wouldn't mind going with me?"

It thrilled him, because it sounded as if she really wanted him to come. "To buy some outfits for my expectant wife? I've been looking forward to this moment since the day we married."

She bit her lip. "Me, too. There's a darling maternity shop I remember passing."

If he knew his wife, throughout their marriage she'd probably gone in it to look around while they'd both been waiting for the news that she was pregnant. She'd been so brave over all these months, submitting to the procedure. As disappointed as he was each time they found out she wasn't pregnant, it was her pain that had killed him. He'd felt so helpless knowing there were no words to bring her the comfort she needed.

"Let's do it. We'll eat lunch afterward."

"I was hoping you'd say that. Maybe there's something wrong with me that I'm always so hungry."

He frowned. "I'm sure there isn't, but to be wise, let's make an appointment for you to see your doctor in Athens on Tuesday, after our counseling session. If a problem did come up, he needs to know you are pregnant and living in Greece for an undetermined period."

Leandros was getting good at tempering his words so he wouldn't come across as harassing her for a commitment she wasn't ready to give.

"Actually, I saw him the day I flew in."

That came as a surprise.

"I wanted to thank him and let him know the procedure finally worked. I'm sure it made him happy."

"Did you tell him we were getting divorced?"

"Yes. I heard the sadness when he said he was very sorry. He told me to call him anytime...." Her voice trailed off, as if she had something else on her mind. "Give me a minute to change my blouse and freshen up."

"Take your time. I'll meet you at the car."

CHAPTER NINE

AFTER A SHOPPING SPREE that resulted in taking home a couple of loose fitting sundresses, plus three new tops and jeans that allowed for growth, Leandros put the purchases in the car and treated Kellie to a delicious lunch.

When she couldn't eat another bite, she lifted her eyes to her husband. "I ate too much, but it tasted so good."

His white smile turned her heart over. "Do you know this vacation is putting weight back on me?"

She studied his handsome features. "It's done it to both of us." He'd looked gaunt when she'd surprised him in his office last week, but with regular meals and rest, he'd started filling out. No man was more gorgeous than Leandros.

"Do you want to go home, or would you like to stretch your legs for a while longer?"

"There's a cute children's shop down on the

other corner. If you don't mind, I'd like to pick up an outfit for Demi before we go back to the villa. Fran says she's growing fast. I imagine she needs the nine-to-twelve-months' size."

"I'm ready when you are." He put some bills on the table and they left the restaurant.

Kellie walked alongside her husband, realizing she had absolutely nothing to complain about. He was his affable, charming self, and he went along with everything she suggested, but a vital spark was missing from his normally vibrant personality.

Every day since her return to Greece, she'd been more and more aware of it. She felt as if she was living with a whitewashed version of the dynamic lover she'd married. All the color seemed to have gone out of him.

That's your *fault, Kellie.*

Over the last few days she felt as if they'd unearthed every major problem and now possessed the tools to keep the lines of communication open. But somewhere in the process he'd changed.

Fear clutched at her to think that the problems in their marriage had done something irreparable to him. She knew he loved her. She knew he loved their unborn babies. But he might not feel the same desire for her anymore. Except for cupping her elbow, or steadying her as she got out of the car, he didn't try to touch her or make overtures as a prelude to making love.

She thought back to the first time she'd met him. It had taken only twenty-four hours from the time he'd helped her get her uncle wheeled into the elevator before he'd kissed her sense-less. Kellie would never forget what he told her after he'd finally lifted his head so they could breathe.

"I want you so much, I wish I could bite the heart out of your body. But then I'd never be able to have that experience again, so we need to get married as soon as possible. Don't tell me you don't want the same thing. I've got you in my arms and can feel your heart leap-ing to reach mine."

"I'm not denying it." She'd half gasped the words while she tried to catch her breath.

"Not everyone experiences the intense de-sire we feel for each other. It's a precious gift we don't dare lose, Kellie, or neither of us will ever be happy again."

A tremor shook her body when she remem-bered that incredible night and her passion-ate response.

Yet the month before she'd left him, she'd

been too distrustful and angry to turn to him for the intimacy she'd always craved. It seemed it had been years since they'd made love. The more he'd tried to love her physically, the more she'd pushed him away.

What if he'd done the same thing to her?

But he hadn't! No matter how bad things had gotten, he'd always reached for her in bed. *She* was the one who'd moved into the guest bedroom and had made plans to vacation with Fran.

Rejection like that could be too painful to forget. Leandros was the total opposite of a spiteful person, but if he didn't crave her affection in the same way anymore, it was because she'd killed something inside him.

Last night he'd gone to bed when his parents did. Their presence had never inhibited him before if he'd wanted to be alone with her. Since her return, he'd had every opportunity to come into her bedroom, whether they were at the Cassandra or on Andros.

All these thoughts were torturing her as they shopped for Demi's gift. The whole time they were in there, he didn't suggest they pick out something for their babies. Her old husband would have bought out the store for them by now.

As the clerk wrapped their gift of an adorable pink top and shorts, Kellie felt a blackness descend. This was how all the pain and suffering had started before. She'd let her fears develop into giant problems without sharing them with Leandros.

What was the expression about not learning lessons from the past, or mankind was destined to repeat the mistakes? Suddenly Mrs. Lasko's warning filled her mind.

"Surely today has given you your first inkling of where to dig to start finding understanding. You'll have to be brutally honest, open up and listen to each other. You'll be forced to wade through perceptions, whether false or accurate, and no matter how painful, arrive at the truth."

It came to Kellie that the problems of trying to get pregnant and the disappointment each time it didn't happen had blown up all the other problems until there was no more communication. Now she was dealing with another inner conflict, one she had to step up and face.

What if she girded up her courage and asked him outright how he felt right now?

Why was it so hard?

What was her greatest fear?

That he'll tell you the truth, that his desire for you has waned.

Was she brave enough to hear the truth from his lips? If she wasn't, then she'd learned nothing from therapy.

They left the shop and went back to the car. As they were leaving the town, they passed the church where they'd been married. On impulse, she turned to him. "Leandros? Would you pull over to the curb for a minute?"

He shot her a concerned glance and immediately found a parking space. "What's wrong? You went quiet on me in the shop. Aren't you feeling well?"

"That's not it," she assured him. "I feel fine, but I realize I haven't been in the church since we took our vows. I only want to go inside for a moment."

A puzzled look broke out on his face. "Why?"

"It's one of my whims. Will you humor me? I've been getting them a lot lately. Do you know, while we were planning our wedding, one of your family members mentioned you and Petra had been married on Andros and—"

"And you assumed this was the church." He ground out the words.

"Yes. I'm sorry to have to admit it was another one of my false assumptions."

He shut off the engine. "Do you want me to go in with you?"

Yes, yes, yes. "If you'd like to."

"I would have brought you here whenever you wanted, but you never expressed a desire. If I'd had my wits about me, I would have asked you to tell me why."

She shook her head. "I wouldn't have told you the real reason. Not then. As for now, I'd like to see it again, knowing you didn't marry Petra in here. Let's face it. I had more than one veil over my eyes on our wedding day."

"I was blinded by the wonder of you."

Leandros.

He came around and helped her out of the car. They walked across the cobblestones to the entrance. The beautiful white church with the latticelike windows had two of the Cycladic, blue-topped spires.

A few people were inside as they entered the nave. Kellie looked around, marveling over the paintings on the walls and ceiling. He escorted her past columns to the front, where they'd stood before an icon of the Virgin to become man and wife.

His gray eyes searched hers for a heart

stopping moment. "What do you remember about that day?" he whispered.

"Being terrified I'd make a mistake in front of all your family and friends," she whispered back. "What about you?"

His features sobered. "I couldn't believe you'd agreed to become my wife. Throughout the ceremony, which I confess was mostly a blur to me, I prayed you wouldn't back out at the last minute."

"You truly worried about that?" She couldn't fathom it. Not Leandros of all people.

"I chased you from the moment we met. You were such an elusive creature, you'll never know the relief I felt when the priest finally made you mine."

Kellie was bemused by his answer. "So I was yours, eh?" she teased.

"Yes," he declared savagely.

Emotion almost closed her throat. "I was so in love with you, I feared you couldn't possibly love me the same way. What had I done to earn such a man's love?"

"Don't you think I asked the same question about you? How come this wonderful, beautiful American woman had agreed to marry me?"

"All I know is I got my heart's desire." Her

pulse rate sped up before she grasped his hands. "Two years have gone by and with them a lot of history. Now it seems the tables have turned and I'm the one chasing you."

At first she didn't think he'd gotten the full import of her words. Not until she saw his chest rise and fall, and felt his fingers tighten around hers.

"We're standing before God. If you lie to me, He'll know it and so will I. So I'm going to ask you a question. Leandros Roussos Petralia—do you still want me in all the ways a man wants a woman? You know what I mean."

A sound like ripping silk came out of him.

"Cat got your tongue? Remember, you're under oath."

He looked tortured. "Kellie...what's going on?"

"If you think about it hard enough, it should come to you."

Removing her hands gently from his, she walked out of the church to the car without looking back.

Leandros grabbed hold of the last pew to steady himself. He didn't know what to think. Kellie was the kind of passionate lover a man would kill for, but she'd never taken the initiative with him in their marriage, not verbally or physically. It had always rested on him.

Therapy had taught him she'd been too insecure all her life to say the words and reach out to him first, of her own accord. But if he'd read her correctly just now, she'd done something unprecedented by letting him know with words she *wanted* him. They hadn't even been to their next therapy session.

Maybe it had taken being in this holy place, with no associations of Petra, for her to find the courage. He was blown away to realize she wanted to sleep with him again. But this didn't necessarily mean she was ready for the final step to get back together.

In a sense he felt fragmented. Part of him couldn't wait to get her home alone. Yet another part feared that once he'd made love to her again, and then she decided she couldn't live with him, after all, he wouldn't be able to handle the pain. One night with her would never be enough.

Before he made a fatal mistake and temporarily assuaged his longing, only to find out there would never be another time, they had more talking to do. With a mixture of elation and terror, he left the church and joined her in the car. She didn't look at him as he started the engine.

Once they were on the road, he glanced at her profile. "To answer your question, I want you a hundred times more now than I did on our wedding night. If I haven't touched you, you know the reason why."

"That's all I need to hear."

"Kellie—you could have no comprehension of how I felt in the church just now when you let me know you wanted me. Those are the words I've dreamed of hearing you say, but never expected the moment to happen. You've changed from your former self into a woman I hardly recognize."

That brought her head around, causing the golden strands to swish against her shoulders. "I'm sorry you've had to wait so long for me to say the words in my heart," she said with tears in her voice.

"I'm not," he replied. "The wait has made them all the sweeter. Your bravery has emboldened me to ask the one question still unanswered for me. Do you want to call off the divorce? I never wanted it. When you told me you were leaving me..." He gripped the steering wheel harder.

She reached over to touch his arm. "It sounds

like you expect me to spell it out, so I will. I don't want a divorce."

"Thank God."

"Deep inside, whether I was consciously aware of it or not, I know I flew to Athens to get my marriage back. Our precious babies were an excuse to face you after all the terrible things I'd done to you. But that version of me is gone, Leandros. You're beholding the new me, who's ready to love you like you've never been loved before. How am I doing on answering your question so far?"

He could hardly breathe. "Just keep talking until we reach the villa."

"I adore you, Leandros. I always have. You're my whole world, my whole life! I couldn't bear that we were having problems."

"Tell me about it." He half groaned the words.

"It didn't seem possible to me that you could be such a loving husband, and yet be carrying on behind my back with your sister-in-law. Nothing made sense, but I didn't know how to deal with it."

"You weren't alone."

"I have something else to tell you. I spoke with my aunt and uncle for a long time last night."

The information was coming at him like a meteor shower. He could scarcely take it all in.

"The bottom line is, they're going to move into your uncle Manny's villa just as soon as we can arrange it. As you know, Aunt Sybil was always against relocating to Greece because of her worries for Uncle Jim's health. But I got them both on the phone so she couldn't answer for him.

"It would have warmed your heart to hear him tell us how much he loves you and how crazy he is about the idea of a new adventure. After I explained that your dad would love a fishing partner to go out with every morning, my uncle got excited. He told my aunt he didn't want to miss out on one day of watching their grandchildren grow up. My aunt broke down in tears of happiness. I think we can get Frank to help them here until we find a permanent replacement for him."

Speechless, Leandros grasped her hand and clung to it.

"I wonder what Olympia will say at our next session."

The blood pounded in his ears. "She'll tell us to go slowly."

"I know. And she'll ask questions we haven't thought of."

"That's good. She's been pivotal in helping us see into ourselves. I'd like to keep going to her so we'll stay on track."

Kellie squeezed Leandros's fingers. "So would I. Later on we'll have to send her the right gift to show our gratitude. I'm going to have to think about it for a while, but I can't think while I'm sitting next to you, dying to be in your arms.

"When we get back home, I want to go out on our cabin cruiser. I'll pack the food we love. We're going to need a couple of days and nights to get reacquainted, without anyone else around."

Leandros was already thinking a month at least.

"Be warned, I plan to ravish you before I grow as big as a house!"

He laughed with joyous abandon.

"Then I plan to love you to death and never let you go back to work, but that would make you unhappy."

"You don't really think that—"

"I really do. So in a few days you should fly to Athens and do what you do best, by running the Petralia Corporation. Frato is trying to pull his weight, bless his heart, but I happen to know every man and woman in the company is holding their collective breath until you're back at the helm."

His natural impulse was to speed the rest of the way home so he could crush her in his arms, but the instinct to protect his family was stronger and had come out in full force. His wife had finally come back to him, and their babies were growing inside her. What more could a man ask for?

The second he pulled up to the villa, he hurried around to Kellie's side of the car. She already had the door open and flew into his arms, almost knocking him over. "Kiss me, darling," she cried, lifting her mouth to find his. "Don't ever stop."

There was no space between them as they tried to assuage their great longing for each other. His wife was vibrantly alive, kissing away the shadows. Every touch and caress, every breath filled his mind and body with indescribable ecstasy.

He carried her into the house and followed her down on the bed with his body. But he was careful with her as they found old ways and new to bring each other the pleasure denied them for so long, while they'd been sorting out their lives.

It was evening before they lay sated for

a while, their legs entwined, simply enjoying the luxury of looking at each other and being at peace. "The first time we swam together and made love, you reminded me of a painting of the famous Spanish artist Luis Falero. It was called *A Sea Nymph*. She's appearing above the waves with her body submerged. Very enticing. I was taken with it at first glance."

Her smile lit up his insides. "Why didn't you ever tell me?"

"Because you'd never been intimate with a man before and you were easily embarrassed."

She kissed his lips. "But now that I'm with children—*yours*, as a matter of fact—you think I can handle it."

"I think if you saw it, you'd blush, as you do so charmingly. But that was over two years ago and pregnancy has changed you."

"Is that right."

"In the most incredibly gorgeous ways." He pressed a long, hard kiss to her tempting mouth. "Falero did another painting called *The Planet Venus*. The centerpiece is a goddess with flowing gold tresses, very much like you, in fact. After studying you now, I believe his model was in the early stages of her pregnancy. I was always drawn to it."

"I had no idea you were such a lover of nudes."

"Admirer of many, lover of *one*," he corrected, provoking a gentle laugh from her.

"Well…" she eyed him playfully "…since this is confession time, while you were lounging on the sand after we'd made love, it was like the *Reclining Dionysos* on the Parthenon had come to life before my eyes. He's quite spectacular."

Leandros laughed again. "That's not fair. He's missing some of his parts."

She brushed her hand across his well-defined chest. "Everything important is still there." Suddenly the teasing was gone. She leaned over him. "I love you so much, Leandros. Make love to me again. I'm on fire for you and am feeling insatiable."

"That makes two of us, *agapa mou*."

CHAPTER TEN

"CONGRATULATIONS, MRS. PETRALIA. You've reached your thirty-fifth week and all is well with your little boys. Most patients with twins deliver between now and thirty-seven weeks. Since I can predict your babies are going to come earlier than the desired forty weeks for a single baby, I want you to be especially observant of what's going on with your body."

"What *isn't* going on?" she exclaimed. "Last week, when we told our marriage therapist we wanted another appointment with her, to talk about how to be parents to twins, I told her I was as big as a house. I don't think she believed me until she saw me. Secretly, I'm afraid Leandros compares me to a giant walrus." Dr. Hanno burst into laughter. "It's true. That's exactly how I feel."

"It won't be long now. Those menstrual-like cramps you've experienced are normal. So is the lower back pain and uterine pressure.

Sometimes you can't tell if you're having contractions. You'll need to listen to your body very carefully from here on out. My advice is to stay off your feet for a few hours every day to avoid that pressure."

"You mean my swollen stumps?" she quipped. "I can't even bend over to see them."

"Be sure you're still getting the equivalent of four glasses of milk a day. Any questions before you leave?"

"Yes. How do I help my husband to calm down? He's known for being a tour de force in the corporate world, but you wouldn't know it if you lived with him."

The doctor grinned. "There's no cure for what he's got except to have those babies."

"I realize that. Half the time he watches me like a hawk. If I yawn or sigh, he asks me what's wrong. When I get up in the night lately to go to the bathroom, he's pacing on the patio off our bedroom. I'm glad he has to go to work! But throughout his day, he phones every few hours. His parents and my aunt and uncle are a stone's throw away from our villa, but nothing seems to ease his mind. Every night he comes home from work with a new toy or outfit. At this rate we're not going to have room for the babies."

Dr. Hanno eyed her speculatively. "I'm sure you know how lucky you are. Too many women don't have a husband, and even if they do, he's not like yours."

Tears filled her eyes. "I know. I'm very blessed. The hardest thing about the end of this pregnancy is trying to help him not get too worried. His first wife was killed in a plane crash, and she was pregnant. I'm sure those demons are haunting him right now."

"What about your marriage counselor? Maybe the two of you should ask her."

"That's a brilliant idea, but I don't think he'd want to. I'm afraid I'm going to have to talk to him and get him to admit what's driving his heightened anxiety. I'll have to find a creative way to reach him. Thanks for everything, Dr. Hanno."

"I'll see you in three days."

"If not before?" She was so tired of being pregnant, it would be wonderful for it to all be over.

"Maybe."

That *maybe* gave her hope. She left his examination room and walked out to the reception area mentally revitalized.

Her aunt had been reading a magazine.

When she saw Kellie, she put it down and got to her feet. "How are you doing?"

"Just great. He wants to see me in three days."

"You'll probably be going into labor soon."

"I think so, too."

"Let's get you back to the hotel and order a meal. Before long Leandros will be through with work and we'll fly back to Andros."

"He'll be waiting to hear how my appointment went. I'll call him from the limo."

When they left the building, the temperature outside was 56 degrees, typical for February. Kellie had been hot for months and loved the cool air. There'd been a little rain on their way to the doctor's office, but it had stopped.

As soon as she got in the back of the car with her aunt, she phoned Leandros. He picked up after the first ring. "Kellie?" On a scale of one to ten, his anxiety was a hundred.

"Hi, darling. The doctor said everything looks great. I have to keep my legs up for a few hours a day, but otherwise we're ready to go."

"That's the news I've been waiting for. I'll be leaving the office in twenty minutes. Where are you right now?"

"In the limo."

"You're going straight to the hotel, right?"

"Yes. We'll be there in a few minutes."

"I love you." The tone of his deep voice permeated to her insides, thrilling her.

"I love you, too."

"I've decided this is going to be my last day of work." *Oh, help!* "I've had Frato here in the office. He's going to take over for me starting tomorrow morning. I can't concentrate anymore. Mrs. Kostas told me to go home and not come back."

No doubt he'd been driving her crazy, too. Kellie laughed, resigned to the fact that she was going to have her nervous husband around day and night until the big event. "That's marvelous news. I'll see you shortly." She hung up.

Her aunt smiled. "What was that laugh about?"

"Leandros informed me he won't be going to work anymore until after the babies are born."

"Oh, dear."

They both laughed. "I've got to come up with a project for him that will keep him busy for hours at a time."

"I know just the thing. I want to have some window boxes built on the east side of the house."

"Perfect! I'll send him with you to pick things out. With Uncle Jim directing traffic, it ought to keep his mind occupied for one day, anyway." More laughter ensued.

The limo pulled to a stop in front of the Cassandra. Kellie thanked the driver and they both got out. She took two steps on the pavement and felt her sandal slide in a tiny pool of water. The next thing she knew, she was sitting on the ground, having landed with a hard thud. Talk about a beached walrus that wasn't going anywhere.

"Are you all right, honey?" her aunt cried.

"I think so. I feel like an idiot, but I'm thankful I didn't take you down with me."

"You're not in pain?"

"No." She started to get up.

"Let me help."

"Thanks," she whispered. But the moment she stood, she felt moisture run down her legs in a gush. It wasn't from the pool. "Aunt Sybil? My water just broke."

"Hang on to me, honey. I'll call the driver and tell him to come back."

Within a minute, the limo returned. Kellie climbed in while her aunt told the driver they needed to get straight to the hospital.

"Tell him not to phone Leandros. I'll do it or he'll freak out completely."

"Agreed."

She was starting to have pains that were different than what she'd experienced now and then. Her stomach grew rock-hard. The contractions were starting. While they drove to the hospital, she reached in her purse for her cell and phoned Leandros.

"Kellie?"

"Hi, darling. There's been a change in plans. My water just broke and I'm in the limo on the way to the hospital. Our babies are coming." Her voice wobbled. "I'll meet you at the hospital."

"I'll be there in five minutes." His line went dead.

Leandros, masked and gowned, sat next to Kellie while he watched the miracle of their firstborn son's birth. The baby had a tuft of black hair, and according to the pediatrician attending him, he weighed in at six pounds two ounces and was twenty-one inches long.

The excitement in the birthing room was palpable. Leandros didn't know he could be this happy.

"Here comes number two, slick as a whistle." The doctor lifted their second son by the ankles. Again they all heard the healthy infant cry announcing his arrival in the world. Leandros felt pure joy in every atom of his body. "You've got yourselves another beautiful boy. How are you doing, Mom?"

Tears streamed down Kellie's face as she beamed at Leandros. "I'm afraid I might die from so much happiness. Are our babies really all right?"

"They're perfect," he whispered before leaning over to kiss her lips gently.

An army of staff filled the birthing room. The other pediatrician turned his head toward them. "Baby number two weighs in at five pounds fourteen ounces and measures twenty and a half inches. You've given birth to healthy fraternal twins. Congratulations."

In a few minutes they'd been washed and wrapped so Kellie could hold them in her arms. "Oh, darling," she wept. "Our babies..." She kissed their heads. "They're gorgeous, just like you."

Leandros was so full of emotion, he had to wipe his eyes to get a good look. "I can see your beautiful features in both of them. Just think. You and I grew up as only children. They'll always have each other."

"I know. Isn't it wonderful?" But her eyes had closed.

Alarmed, Leandros looked at the doctor. "Is she all right?"

"I've given her a hypo. She'll sleep for several hours. Why don't you go down to the nursery with your sons and get acquainted with them."

After kissing his wife's flushed cheek, he watched the nurses put the babies in carts, and followed them down the hall to the newborn unit. For the next half hour he had the time of his life, examining every finger and toenail. Their sons had made it. His wife had made it. A wave of love for her, for their offspring, swept through him, shaking him to the very foundations.

When he finally went out into the hall, he saw everyone standing at the glass—his parents, her aunt and uncle, Fran and Nik. The celebration could probably be heard throughout the wing. His mother flung herself into his arms and sobbed. As for his father, he was so choked up he couldn't talk.

Leandros leaned down to give Jim a hug, then swept Sybil into his arms. All everyone did was cry. Fran was no different. She gave him a giant hug. "Hallelujah this day has come," she whispered.

Then it was Nik's turn to give him the mother of bear hugs. "Sybil told us you're on vacation now. Believe me, you're going to need it with all those two o'clock feedings. I couldn't be happier for you, Leandros."

"I feel like *I've* given birth. I can't even imagine what Kellie's feeling like."

"She's blissfully knocked out."

"You're right." He chuckled. "Thanks for being here."

"We wouldn't be anywhere else. Have you decided on names?"

"We did as soon as we found out we were having boys. We decided the first one to come out would be Nikolas Vlassius Petralia."

Nik's eyes grew suspiciously bright. "You're kidding me."

"I swear I'm not. Kellie was adamant about it. She loves you like a brother. I think you know that by now."

"I'm honored," he said in a croaky voice. "What will you call your other son?"

"Dimitri Milo Petralia in honor of her uncle Jim, who was the perfect father to her all her life, and of course her birth father."

"Does Jim know that yet?"

"We had dinner for everyone last week and told them."

"The Petralia brothers, Nik and Dimitri. That has a definite ring."

Leandros had to admit that it did. After they were born, he'd told Kellie what it meant to him to have sons. She'd kissed him and said, "Don't you think I know that? Don't you know how I watched you suffer each time we knew we weren't pregnant? It almost killed me to see your pain. After all, you're a proud Greek male. I'm just thankful you finally got your heart's desire."

"One day our children will be playing with your Demi."

"They grow up fast. You've done great work, Leandros."

"I give all the credit to my angel wife. She's the one who got us into counseling and saved our marriage."

Nik shook his head. "I'm convinced you would have made your way back to each other no matter what. I shudder to think that if she hadn't phoned Fran to come to Greece…"

Leandros patted his good friend on the shoulder. "You would have met Fran at a later date. When you consider the if's, it makes you realize it was all meant to be."

* * *

At 6:00 p.m. Kellie tiptoed into the nursery to check on the babies one more time. They'd both been fed and burped. Now they were sound asleep. She got a swelling in her chest. They were the dearest babies on earth, and that wasn't just because she was their mother. Their Petralia genes made them beautiful.

She looked down at each one, feasting her eyes on their darling faces and bodies. The sky-blue of their little sleepers with feet brought out their dark hair and olive skin, just a few of Leandros's striking assets. They bore a strong resemblance to each other, but there were distinct differences she was happy about.

Kellie wanted them each to grow up being their own person. Leandros felt the same way. It would be fun to play up the twin thing once in a while, but it was important they had their own identities.

They were seven weeks old today. She remembered back to the time when Dr. Creer had told her she was pregnant and seven weeks along. "Big as blueberries," he'd said. Children had brought a whole new meaning to her life.

Lately she'd found herself thinking a lot about her parents. Unquestionably, they would have loved Kellie the same way. What a lucky girl she'd been to be raised by her aunt and uncle, whom she looked upon as her heroes. They'd not only raised her, they were now helping her and Leandros raise the children.

With everyone in both families pitching in, the exciting, chaotic and exhausting experience of having twins hadn't been quite as overwhelming as she would have imagined. Fran and Nik had spent several weekends with them. With their precious Demi walking around, getting into everything she could touch, while the babies lay on the floor watching her, they had hilarious times.

"Good night, my darlings," she whispered. "Forgive me if I don't see you for the next twenty-four hours, but I've got special plans for your father he doesn't know about. All these weeks he's been waiting on you and me. Now he needs some personal attention. Both your grandmas will be taking care of you until we come back tomorrow night. Be good for them. I'll miss you." She kissed each one and tiptoed out of the nursery.

Thea and Sybil were settled in the living room watching television. Kellie walked over to give them each a hug. "I'm leaving now. Call us if there's an emergency."

Her aunt nodded. "Of course. Now you go on. If you don't come back for a week, we won't mind, will we, Thea?"

"We wish you *would* stay away more than twenty-four hours."

"I couldn't bear to be separated from them that long. And you know Leandros. He's so crazy about them, I'm not sure he'll last until tomorrow night."

The two women gave each other a knowing smile, causing Kellie's cheeks to go warm. "Thank you from the bottom of my heart." She blew them a kiss, then let herself out the front door into the April evening. The helicopter would be bringing him home from work any minute. Her plan was to be there the moment he jumped out.

She was wearing a new pair of jeans and a short-sleeved, oatmeal-colored cotton sweater he'd never seen before. Though she still had ten pounds to lose, she'd gone down enough sizes to fit into non-maternity clothes. To her satisfaction, she could tuck in the sweater. She wanted to make sure he knew she was getting her shape back. He liked her hair long, so she'd left it loose after blow drying it. A little perfume, lipstick and makeup did wonders for her spirits.

When she heard the helicopter coming, she began to tremble, anticipating the night to come. Two weeks ago she'd had a checkup. The doctor told her she could have relations with her husband at seven weeks. Tonight was the night, only Leandros didn't know it yet.

She hid behind a tree until the helicopter touched down and Leandros got out. He spoke with the pilot for a few minutes, then started down the path to their villa, throwing his suit coat over his shoulder. She sneaked up behind him and wrapped her arms around his waist, clutching him tightly against her.

"Don't turn around if you know what's good for you. Do everything I say, and you won't get hurt."

His shoulders started to shake with silent laughter. "Don't I even get a peek?"

"You talk too much, Mr. Petralia. Just keep walking down to the pier. I'm right behind you."

He went along with her little game and began walking. "What do I do when I get there?"

"We're going sailing. Just you and me."

"It'll be dark soon."

"We don't have to set sail tonight. We can wait until morning."

"That's good, because I'm starving."

"I plan to feed you."

"I'll need a shower first."

"That's all been arranged."

They reached the dock where her sailboat was tied up. She'd spent part of the afternoon making the bed and getting things ready belowdecks. After going to the store, she'd stocked the fridge with his favorite goodies. On her final trip, she'd brought down his toiletries and laid out a new robe for him. He wouldn't want for a thing.

"How soon can I turn around?"

"After you go below."

He stepped into the boat. She stepped where he stepped and trailed him down the stairs.

The lights of several dozen votive candles placed around the ledge beckoned him from the small bedroom. He stopped in place when he saw what she'd created. Suddenly he swung around. His eyes blazed as he took in the sight of her. She felt his desire reach out to her like a living thing.

"Kellie—"

"The doctor gave me the seal of approval. I thought it was about time the man who holds my heart was paid a little attention for a change. Tonight there's no one but you and me. I'm dying to make love to you, Leandros."

"You look so beautiful, I'm staggered."

"Good. Now you know how I feel every time I get near you. What would you like to do first?"

"I want to devour you over and over again," he said in a husky voice. "Come here to me, darling."

Kellie didn't need those words to reach for him. His mouth was life to her. The touch of his hands on her body was a revelation to her. They fell on the bed, desperate for the closeness after having to wait the last two months for this moment.

Hours later they surfaced long enough to eat, then they went back to bed. During the night he pulled her into him. "I think I love you too much," he whispered into her hair. "You have no idea how divine you are."

"You took the words out of my mouth." She kissed his hard jaw. "I got so excited waiting for the helicopter to arrive, I almost had a heart attack."

"I would have come home sooner, but I had three unexpected visitors in my office before I left."

She cupped his face in her hands. "Who?"

"The Paulos family. Karmela has been in therapy for months. She came to apologize."

Kellie sat all the way up. "It must have been so hard for her to face you."

"I'm sure it was, but she did it."

"How is she, darling?"

"There's a definite change in her. She's not on the attack anymore. How much medication plays a role in this new behavior, I don't know, but it's welcome. The day you went to the hospital, she saw the news about our twins on TV. She wanted me to tell you she's very happy for us and sorry for any pain she's caused."

"That's a huge step in the right direction."

"I think so, too."

Kellie nestled against him again. "I'm glad you told me. We can finally leave all that in the past where it belongs, and concentrate on our new lives. I love our boys so much. I love you so much."

"Show me again how much, *agapi mou*. Show me again and again."

* * * * *

COMING NEXT MONTH from Harlequin® Romance

AVAILABLE MAY 7, 2013

2 NOVELS for the PRICE of 1

THIS MONTH ONLY!

#4375 A FATHER FOR HER TRIPLETS

Mothers in a Million

Susan Meier

Missy Johnson worked hard to give her adorable triplets a secure childhood. So when Wyatt McKenzie comes back to town, she realizes five might be the perfect number!

#4376 THE MATCHMAKER'S HAPPY ENDING

Mothers in a Million

Shirley Jump

Matchmaker Marnie Franklin is shocked to meet Jack Knight again. But soon he shows her that her own Mr. Right is right under her nose!

#4377 SECOND CHANCE WITH THE REBEL

Mothers in a Million

Cara Colter

Lucy was devastated when Mac left years ago. But now he's back in town, and charming as ever. Surely everyone deserves a second chance at happiness?

#4378 FIRST COMES BABY...

Mothers in a Million

Michelle Douglas

Ben has been Meg's best friend since childhood. But when he helps her become a mother, can he convince Meg that he's finally ready to settle down?

You can find more information on upcoming Harlequin® titles, free excerpts and more at www.Harlequin.com.

HRLPCNM0413

LARGER-PRINT BOOKS!
GET 2 FREE LARGER-PRINT NOVELS PLUS
2 FREE GIFTS!

HARLEQUIN®

Romance

From the Heart, For the Heart